The Collector's Wodehouse

P. G. WODEHOUSE

Something Fishy

THE OVERLOOK PRESS
WOODSTOCK & NEW YORK

This edition first published in the United States in 2008 by
The Overlook Press, Peter Mayer Publishers, Inc.
Woodstock and New York

WOODSTOCK
One Overlook Drive
Woodstock, NY 12498
www.overlookpress.com
[for individual orders, bulk and special sales, contact our Woodstock office]

NEW YORK
141 Wooster Street
New York, NY 10012

First published in the US by Simon and Schuster, New York, 1957
under the title *The Butler Did It*
Copyright by The Trustees of the Wodehouse Estate
All rights reserved

Cataloging-in-Publication Data is available from the Library of Congress

Manufactured in Germany

ISBN 978-1-59020-068-1

1 3 5 7 9 8 6 4 2

Something Fishy

The dinner given by J. J. Bunyan at his New York residence on the night of September the tenth, 1929, was attended by eleven guests, most of them fat and all, except Mortimer Bayliss, millionaires. In the pre-October days of the year 1929 you seldom met anyone in New York who was not a millionaire. He might be a little short of the mark when you ran into him on Monday morning, but by Friday afternoon he would have got the stuff all right and be looking around for more. Not one of those present but had made his hundred thousand dollars or so in the past few hours, and no doubt Keggs, Mr Bunyan's English butler, and the rest of the Park Avenue staff had added appreciably to their savings, as in all probability had the two chauffeurs, the ten gardeners, the five stablemen and the pastry cook down at Meadowhampton, Long Island, where Mr Bunyan had his summer home.

For the bull market was booming and the golden age had set in with a roll of drums and a fanfare of trumpets. About the only problem worrying people in those happy days was what to do with all the easy money which a benevolent Providence kept pouring so steadily out of its cornucopia all the time.

It was to this subject that the company's attention had turned when dinner was over and Keggs had withdrawn his stately presence and left them to their cigars and coffee, and the debate was in full swing when Mortimer Bayliss intervened in it. For the last ten minutes he had been sitting hunched up in his chair, scowling silently and curling a scornful lip.

Mortimer Bayliss was the curator of the world-famous Bunyan picture collection. Mr Bunyan liked having him as a guest at these otherwise all-financier dinners, partly because he felt he lent an intellectual tone but principally because he made a speciality of being abominably rude to everyone except his employer, which appealed to the latter's primitive sense of humour. Mortimer Bayliss was a tall, thin, sardonic man who looked like a Mephistopheles troubled with ulcers, and he had the supercilious manner which so often renders art experts unpopular. He considered his fellow diners clods and Philistines and their foolish babble offended him.

'Yachts!' he said. 'Palaces on the Riviera! Oh God, oh Montreal. Have you wretched embryos no imagination? Get some fun out of your beastly wealth, why don't you?'

'How do you mean, fun?' asked one of the stouter millionaires.

'I mean do something that will give you an interest in life.' Mortimer Bayliss flashed a black-rimmed monocle about the table and glared through it at a harmless little man who looked like an overfed rabbit. 'You!' he said. 'Brewster or whatever your name is. Ever heard of Tonti?'

'Sure. He wrote a song called "Good-bye".'

'That was Tosti, my poor oaf. Tonti was an Italian banker who flourished in the seventeenth century and in the intervals of telling people that it would be impossible in the circumstances to sanction an increase in their overdraft invented the tontine. And if you want me to tell you what a tontine is—'

'I know that,' said J. J. Bunyan. 'It's where a bunch of guys put up money and found a trust and the money goes on accumulating till they all die off and there's only one fellow left in, and he takes the lot. Right?'

'Correct in every detail, J. J. You and I are educated men.'

'Somebody once wrote a story about a tontine.'

'Robert Louis Stevenson. Title, *The Wrong Box*.'

'That's right. Remember enjoying it as a kid.'

'You had good taste. Have any of you untutored peasants read *The Wrong Box*? No? I thought as much. I don't suppose you read anything except the *Wall Street Journal* and *Captain Billy's Whizz Bang*. Just a mob of barely sentient illiterates,' said Mortimer Bayliss, and helped himself to another glass of the cognac which his medical adviser had warned him on no account to touch.

'What made you bring Tonti up, Mort?' said J. J. Bunyan. 'Are you suggesting that we start a tontine?'

'Why not? Don't you think it would be fun?'

'It might, at that.'

The man who had been addressed as Brewster wrinkled his brow. It always took him some time to assimilate anything not having to do with figures.

'I don't get the idea, J. J. What happens? Suppose we each put up a thousand dollars—'

'A thousand?' Mortimer Bayliss snorted. 'Fifty thousand is more like it. You want to make it interesting, don't you?'

'All right, fifty thousand. Then what?'

'You die – a task well within the scope of even your abilities. You die off one by one, and when you've all died except one, that one scoops the kitty. J. J. explained it a moment ago in his admirably lucid way, but apparently it did not penetrate the concrete. That's the worst of those cheap imitation heads, they're never satisfactory.'

A millionaire with high blood pressure took a dim view of the suggestion. He said it sounded to him like waiting for dead men's shoes, and Mortimer Bayliss said that that was precisely what it was.

'I don't like it.'

'Tonti did.'

'Sounds sort of gruesome to me. And another thing. The winner wouldn't collect till he was about ninety, and what use would the money be to him then? Silly, I call it.'

Six other millionaires said it seemed silly to them, too.

'The voting appears to be against you, Mort,' said J. J. Bunyan. 'Try again.'

'How about your sons?'

'How do you mean, how about them?'

'You've all got sons, and pretty repulsive most of them are. Start a tontine for them. No, wait,' said Mortimer Bayliss, a finger to his forehead. 'Here's a really bright idea. Just came to me, born no doubt of this potent brandy. Start a tontine for your revolting offspring, but fix it that the cash goes to the one that's the last to get married. Same thing, really. Death or marriage, what's the difference?' said Mortimer Bayliss, who had been a bachelor for forty-three years and intended to remain one.

This time his audience was far more responsive. There were murmurs of interest and approval. Quick-witted millionaires could be heard explaining the thing to neighbours whose brains moved more slowly.

'If you each put in fifty thousand, that's over half a million to begin with, and—'

'Compound interest,' said J. J. Bunyan, rolling the words round his tongue like vintage port.

'Exactly. There will be the interest piling up over the years.

By the time the money's paid out it should come to close on a million. Worth having, that, and the most you stand to lose is your original stake, which you're going to lose anyway when this bull market explodes, as it most certainly will. What was it someone said of the Roman Empire in the days of Tiberius? "It is too large, a bubble blown so big and tenuous that the first shock will disrupt it in suds." That's what's going to happen here. There's a crash coming, my hearties, a crash that'll shake the fillings out of your back teeth and dislocate your spinal cords.'

Shocked voices rose in protest. Mortimer Bayliss was a licensed buffoon, but this was carrying buffoonery too far. Even J. J. Bunyan pursed his lips.

'Really, Mort!'

'All right. I'm just telling you. Shoot, if you must, this old grey head, but these things will come to pass. I have read it in the tea leaves. My little bit of money is safely tucked away in government bonds, and I advise you to put yours there. With every stock on the list quoted at about ten times its proper value, there's got to be a crash sooner or later. That's why I suggest that you start this tontine for your progeny. Then at least one of the unfortunate little tykes won't have to end his days selling pencils in the street. Of course, there's just one thing. I don't know how far you super-fatted plutocrats trust one another – not an inch, I imagine, and very sensible of you, too – but I have heard that you do observe gentlemen's agreements. Correct, J. J.?'

'Of course it's correct. Nobody here would dream of breaking a gentlemen's agreement.'

'Well, it's obvious that you will have to have a solemn gentlemen's agreement to keep the thing under your hats. Tip the lads off to what they're going to lose by entering the holy state, and you'll have eleven permanent celibates on your hands. Henry the

Eighth and Brigham Young would have stayed single if they had known that listening to the voice of love was going to set them back a million bucks. Well, there you are, that's the best I can do for you,' said Mortimer Bayliss and, having directed a stare of scorn and loathing at the company through his black-rimmed monocle, refilled his glass and sat back, looking like a Mephistopheles who has just placed before a prospective client an attractive proposition involving the sale of his soul.

His words were followed by a silence in which you could have heard a stock drop. It lasted till J. J. Bunyan spoke.

'Boys,' said J. J. Bunyan, 'I think our friend Mort has got something.'

The sunshine of a fine summer morning was doing its best for the London suburb of Valley Fields, beaming benevolently on its tree-lined roads, its neat little gardens, its rustic front gates and its soaring television antennae.

It was worth the sun's while to take a little trouble over Valley Fields, for there are few more pleasant spots on the outskirts of England's metropolis. One of its residents, a Major Flood-Smith, in the course of a letter to the *South London Argus* exposing the hellhounds of the local Rates and Taxes Department, once alluded to it as 'a fragrant oasis'. He gave the letter to his cook to mail, and she forgot it and found it three weeks later in a drawer and burned it, and the editor would never have printed it, anyway, it being diametrically opposed to the policy for which the *Argus* had always fearlessly stood, but – and this is the point we would stress – in using the words 'fragrant oasis' the Major was dead right. He had rung the bell, hit the nail on the head and put the thing in a nutshell.

Where other suburbs go in for multiple stores and roller-skating rinks and Splendide Cinemas, Valley Fields specializes in trees and grass and flowers. More seeds are planted there each spring, more lawn-mowers pushed, more garden-rollers borrowed and more patent mixtures for squirting green fly purchased than in any other community on the Surrey side of the river Thames. This gives it a rural charm which – to quote Major Flood-Smith once more – makes it absolutely damned impossible to believe that you are only seven miles from Piccadilly Circus. (Or, if a crow, only five.) One has the feeling, as one comes out of its olde-worlde station, that this is where Tennyson must have got the idea of the island valley of Avilion, where falls not hail or rain or any snow, nor ever wind blows loudly.

Of all the delectable spots in Valley Fields (too numerous to mention) it is probable that the connoisseur would point with the greatest pride at Mulberry Grove, the little cul-de-sac, bright with lilac, almond, thorn, rowan and laburnum trees, which lies off Rosendale Road, and it was here that the sun was putting in its adroitest work. At the house which a builder with romance in his soul had named Castlewood its rays made their way across the neat garden and passed through french windows into a cosy living-room, where they lit up, among other interesting objects, an aspidistra plant, a cuckoo clock, a caged canary, a bowl of gold fish, the photograph in a silver frame of a strikingly handsome girl, inscribed 'Love, Elaine', and another photograph similarly framed – this one of an elderly gentleman with a long upper lip and beetling eyebrows, who signed himself 'Cordially yours, Uffenham'. Finally, reaching the armchair, they rested on the portly form of Augustus Keggs, retired butler, who was reading *The Times*. The date on the paper was June 20, 1955.

The twenty-five years and nine months which had elapsed since J. J. Bunyan's dinner party had robbed the world of that dinner's host and most of his guests, but they had touched Keggs lightly. For some reason, probably known to scientists, butlers, as far at any rate as outward appearance is concerned, do not grow old as we grow old. Keggs, reclining in his chair with his feet on a foot-stool and a mild cigar between his lips, looked almost precisely as he had looked a quarter of a century ago. Then he had resembled a Roman emperor who had been doing himself too well on the starchy foods. His aspect now was that of a somewhat stouter Roman emperor, one who had given up any attempt to watch his calories and liked his potatoes with lots of butter on them.

So solidly was he wedged into the cushions that one would have said that nothing short of a convulsion of nature would have been able to hoist him out of them. This, however, was not the case. As the door opened and a small, fair-haired girl came in, he did not actually leap to his feet, but he heaved himself up in slow motion like a courtly hippopotamus rising from its bed of reeds on a riverbank. This was Jane Benedick, niece of the Lord Uffenham who, as stated on that photograph, was cordially his. Lord Uffenham, under whom he had served on his return from America in the early thirties, had been the last of his long list of employers.

'Good morning, Mr Keggs.'

'Good morning, miss.'

Jane was a pretty girl – eyes blue, nose small, figure excellent – at whom most men would have cast more than a passing glance, but the really attractive thing about her was her voice, which was one of singular beauty. It sometimes reminded Lord Uffenham, who had his poetical moments, of ice tinkling in a glass of Rockcup.

'I wouldn't have disturbed you,' said Jane, 'but the big shot is screaming for breakfast, and I can't find his *Times* anywhere. Did you pinch it?'

A touch of embarrassment crept into Kegg's manner.

'Yes, miss. I am sorry. I was glancing at the marriage announcements.'

'Any hot news?'

'There was an item of interest to me, miss. I see that Mr James Brewster was married yesterday.'

'Friend of yours?'

'The son of a friend of the gentleman in whose employment I was many years ago in New York.'

'I see. Belonging to your early or American period.'

'I make something of a hobby of following the matrimonial ventures of the sons of Mr Bunyan's friends. Sentiment, I suppose.'

'Does you credit. Bunyan? Any relation of the Roscoe Bunyan who's taken Shipley?'

'His father, miss. A very wealthy gentleman. Like so many others, he lost a great deal of money in the market crash of 1929, but I believe the younger Mr Bunyan inherited a matter of twenty million dollars after paying death duties.'

'Golly! And Uncle George says he haggled about the rent like a shopkeeper in an Oriental bazaar. He isn't married, is he?'

'No, miss.'

'A bit of luck for some nice girl.'

'I have the same feeling, unless he has greatly changed from the days when I was in his father's service. I remember him as a most unpleasant boy.'

'So do I, by golly. What I could tell you about Roscoe Bunyan!'

'You, miss? When did you meet Mr Roscoe?'

'During my early or American period. Didn't you know that I was sent off to America at the beginning of the war with a lot of other children?'

'No, miss. I had retired and was no longer with his lordship some years before hostilities broke out.'

'Well, I was. Uncle George exported me, and I was taken over for the duration by some kind people who went for the summer to a place called Meadowhampton on Long Island. The Bunyan country house was there. Did they have it in your time?'

'Oh, yes, miss. We were at Meadowhampton every year from the middle of June to Labour Day. A charming spot.'

'I'd have liked it a lot better if it hadn't been for Roscoe. He made my life hell, the little brute. Or he did till one of the other boys stopped him. He had a foul habit of ducking me in the pool down on the beach where we all went, and one day after he had held me under water till I swelled like a gasometer and my whole life seemed to pass before my eyes this angel boy told him that if he didn't desist he would knock his block off. So he desisted. But I still dream about him in nightmares. And now after all these years he has popped up in England and evicted me from my childhood home. It's a strange world, Mr Keggs.'

'Most extraordinary.'

'Still, too late to do anything about it now, I suppose,' said Jane. 'Hullo, who's this?'

'Miss?'

Jane was roaming about the room, and had come to the table in the corner.

'This "Love, Elaine" thing. New, isn't it?'

'Yes, miss. I received it yesterday.'

'Who is it?'

'My niece Emma, miss.'

'It says Elaine.'

'She acts under the name of Elaine Dawn.'

'Oh, she's on the stage? I don't wonder, with a face like that. She's beautiful.'

'I believe she is generally admired.'

'Emma Keggs?'

'Billson, miss. Her mother, my sister Flossie, is Mrs Wilberforce Billson.'

As Jane stood there, silenced by the revelation that this superman had a sister called Flossie, and wondering if she called him Gus, there came from outside the sound of ponderous footsteps.

'Uncle George up and about,' she said. 'I must be going and getting that breakfast.'

A shadow flitted across Keggs's ample face. He was able to bear up bravely at the thought of Lord Uffenham, his circumstances reduced by post-war conditions, economizing by living in lodgings in a London suburb, but he had never been able to reconcile himself to the fact of his lordship's niece soiling her hands in the kitchen. Though so much of his butlerhood had been passed in the United States, Augustus Keggs had never lost his ingrained reverence for the aristocracy of his native land.

'I don't like to think of you doing the cooking, miss.'

'Somebody had to take it on when your Mrs Brown became sick of a fever. And you can't say I don't do it well.'

'You do it admirably, miss.'

'I got a lot of practice at home. We always seemed to be a cook short.'

Keggs heaved a nostalgic sigh.

'When I was at Shipley Hall, his lordship had a staff of ten.'

'And now look at him. These are the times that try men's souls.'

'They are, indeed.'

'Still, we're snug enough here. Ought to consider ourselves

jolly lucky, finding a haven like this. If it isn't Shipley, it's the next best thing. You can almost feel you're in the country. All the same, I wish we had a bit more money.'

'It may come from the sale of his lordship's pictures, miss.'

'Oh, you've heard about those?'

'His lordship was telling me last night, as we walked back from the Green Lion. He hopes they will restore the family fortunes.'

'No harm in hoping,' said Jane, and went off to scramble eggs.

For some moments after she had left, Keggs remained wrapped in thought. Then, going to the writing-table, he took from a drawer a leather-covered notebook and turned to a page that contained a list of names. Unscrewing his fountain pen, he proceeded to put a tick against one of them. It was the name of James Barr Brewster, only son of the late John Waldo Brewster of New York City, who on the previous day had been united in matrimony to Sybil, daughter of Colonel and Mrs R. G. Fanshawe-Chadwick of The Hollies, Cheltenham.

Only two names on the list now remained unticked. He went to the telephone. He had no need to ask Information for the number he required. It was graven on his memory.

'Shipley Hall,' said a fruity voice. 'Mr Roscoe Bunyan's residence.'

'Good morning. Could I speak to Mr Bunyan? This is Mr Keggs, his father's former butler.'

The voice at the Shipley end became warmer. Deep was calling to deep, butler to butler.

'Mr Bunyan is in London at the moment, Mr Keggs. He went up yesterday to attend a party. Would you care to speak to Mr Bayliss?'

'No, thank you. It is a personal matter. Mr Mortimer Bayliss, would that be?'

'That's right.'

'He is in England, then?'

'Been staying here about a week. And a weird old duck he is, too.'

Keggs did not encourage this lapse into criticism of an employer's guests. He had his code.

'When,' he asked, with a touch of formal coldness, 'will Mr Bunyan be returning?'

'This morning, he said.'

'If I were to call at about eleven?'

'You'd catch him then, I think.'

'Thank you, Mr—'

'Skidmore.'

'Thank you, Mr Skidmore,' said Keggs, and hung up.

CHAPTER 3

Out in the garden under the shade of a spreading tree, Lord Uffenham, having bathed, shaved and done his daily dozen, had seated himself at a rustic table and was waiting for the ravens to feed him. Beside him on the grass lay a fine bulldog, sunk at the moment in sleep but ready to become alert at the first signs of breakfast. At these alfresco meals he usually found the pickings good.

George, sixth Viscount Uffenham, was a man built on generous lines. It was as though nature had originally intended to make two viscounts, but had decided half-way through to use all the material at one go, and get the thing over with. In shape he resembled a pear, being reasonably narrow at the top but getting wider all the way down and culminating in a pair of boots of the outsize or violin-case type. Above his great spreading steppes of body there was poised a large and egglike head, the bald dome of which rose like some proud mountain peak from a foothill fringe of straggling hair. His upper lip was very long and straight, his chin pointed. Two huge unblinking eyes of the palest blue looked out from beneath rugged brows with a strange fixity. His air was that of a man perpetually thinking deep thoughts, and so indeed he was. His mental outlook closely resembled that of the White Knight in *Through The Looking-Glass*, who, it will be remembered, frequently omitted to hear what was said to him because he was thinking of a way to feed oneself on batter and so go on from day to day getting a little fatter.

'There you are,' said Jane, arriving with laden tray. 'Scrambled eggs, all piping hot, coffee, toast, butter, marmalade, *The Times* and a couple of biscuits for the hound. Well, what's on your mind, baby?'

'Hey?'

'I heard a whirring sound as I approached, and knew it must be your brain working. I hope I haven't derailed a train of cosmic thought.'

'Hey?'

Jane sighed. Conversing with the head of the family often tended to try the patience of his loved ones, for when some matter of import engrossed him he had an annoying habit of going off into a trance and becoming remote. Concentrated now on whatever it was that had engaged his interest, he gave the impression that it would be possible to get into communication with him only on the ouija board. But Jane was a resourceful girl. She took the coffee pot and pressed it firmly on his hand, and he came out of his coma with a yelp of anguish.

'Hey! What's the idea? Lord love a duck, are you aware that that pot is slightly hotter than blazes?'

'Well, I wanted to rouse you. What were you musing about?'

'Hey? Musing? Oh, yer mean musing? I was musing, if yer must know, on Keggs. I've come to the conclusion that Keggs is deep and dark.'

'How do you mean, deep and dark?'

'Subtle. Sinister. Machiavellian. Never suspected it when he was with me at Shipley, no doubt because butlers wear the mask, but now I find myself eyeing him askance and wondering what he'll be up to next. Take that episode at the pub.'

'What episode was that?'

'And look at this Mulberry Grove place. Three houses in it – Castlewood, Peacehaven and The Nook – each with its summer-house, each with its bird bath, and all Keggs property. How, I ask myself, did Augustus Keggs accumulate the money to buy this vast estate? You don't get summerhouses and bird baths for nothing.'

'He bought them with his savings, chump.'

'But how did he acquire those savings?'

'He was years in America before he came to you, working for Mr Bunyan, the father of the frightful young man who's taken Shipley. I suppose the Bunyan home was always full of guests at week-ends, and American week-end guests never tip the butler less than a thousand dollars.'

Lord Uffenham considered this.

'I see what yer mean. Yerss, as you say, that might account for his opulence. Nevertheless, I still maintain, after what happened at the pub, that the blighter is slippery. A twister, if ever there was one.'

'What was it that happened at the pub? You didn't tell me.'

'I did.'

'You didn't.'

'Oh, didn't I? Fully intended to. Must have slipped my mind. It was at the Green Lion in Rosendale Road. He and I looked in there last night for a quick one, and almost before we'd had time to blow the froth off he was chiselling the aborigines out of their hard-earned cash by means of . . . what's the word?'

'What's what word?'

'The word I'm trying to think of. Chick something.'

'Chicanery?'

'That's right, chicanery. You ever been in a pub?'

'No.'

'Well, you all sit around and swig yer beer and discuss whatever subject happens to come up, and it wasn't long before Keggs turned the conversation to boxing. It's a thing he's interested in. His sister married a boxer, he tells me. Feller of the name of Billson. Battling Billson I believe he was called. Retired now, runs a pub somewhere. Lots of these fellers run pubs when they leave the ring. Where was I?'

'Sitting around and swigging yer beer.'

'That's right, and, as I say, Keggs brought up the subject of boxing, deploring the way it had deteriorated. The chaps fighting now, he claimed, weren't a patch on the old timers. "Ah," he said, shaking his bally head in a mournful sort of way, "we haven't any nippy welterweights like Jack Dempsey today."'

'But wasn't Jack Dempsey a heavyweight?'

'Of course he was, and so a dozen voices told him. But he would stick to it that he only weighed ten stone four, and bobs were produced on every side by those who thought they were on a safe thing and placed in the custody of the landlord, who was appointed arbiter. "I'm sorry, Mr Keggs," he said, "but I'm afraid I must decide against you. Jack Dempsey weighed over thirteen stone when he won the heavyweight championship from Jess Willard." And was Keggs taken aback? Not a bit. Did he exhibit pique? Or chagrin? Not a trace. "Oh, *that* Jack Dempsey?" he said with one of those faint, tolerant smiles. "I was not referring to him. Naturally I meant the original Jack Dempsey, the Nonpareil." And he pulled out a book – yerss, he had it in his pocket – and read out where it said about how it is interesting to remember that the fighting weight of Jack Dempsey the Nonpareil was only a hundred and forty-four pounds with tights on. Well, there was a pretty general outcry, as you can imagine, with those present hotly demanding their bobs back, but the landlord had no option but to award the stakes to Keggs, and he cleaned up as much as fifteen shillings and sixpence. He told me, when we were walking home, that he had made a steady income for thirty years out of that piece of chicanery. So now perhaps you'll agree that he's deep and dark and wants watching.'

'I think he's a sweetie-pie.'

'A sweetie-pie, no doubt, in many respects, but a slippery sweetie-pie, the sort of sweetie-pie apt at any moment to be up to something fishy. I wouldn't trust him as far as I could throw . . .' Lord Uffenham looked about him for an illustration. '. . . as far as I could throw that ruddy statue,' he concluded.

The statue in question, standing on the lawn of Peacehaven, the house next door, was what is known in the trade as a colossal nude, and it was the work of a young sculptor named Stanhope Twine, who lived there. Jane – possibly because she was engaged to be married to him – admired it. Lord Uffenham did not. He disliked the statue, and he had no use whatever for Stanhope Twine. The Supreme Being, he presumed, would not have created Stanhope Twine without some definite purpose in view, but as to what that purpose could have been Lord Uffenham frankly confessed himself fogged. He resented being called on to share the same planet with a herring-gutted young son of a what-not who marcelled his hair, wore yellow corduroy trousers and, when he met his elders and betters, said "Ah, Uffenham" to them in an insufferably patronizing tone of voice. Jane always wanted to stroke Stanhope Twine's head. Lord Uffenham would have preferred to beat it in with a hatchet. He looked down with a reproachful eye at the bulldog, whose name, like his own, was

George. This otherwise excellent animal had more than once given signs of wanting to fraternize with Stanhope Twine. He had that defect, so common in bulldogs, of liking everyone, from the highest to the lowest.

Jane was looking at the statue.

'Stanhope thinks it's the best thing he's done,' she said.

'Stanhope!'

'Don't say "Stanhope!"'

'I only said "Stanhope!"'

'But in a cold, soupy voice as if it revolted your lips to frame the word.'

This was precisely how Lord Uffenham's lips had felt about it, but he lacked the nerve to say so. Though a courageous man with a fine military record in his younger days, he feared his niece's wrath. Jane, when the tigress that slept within her was roused, had a nasty way of telling him that something had gone wrong with the kitchen range and there would be only bread and cheese for dinner. Changing the subject tactfully, he said:

'Hey!'

'Yes, m'lord?'

'Did you go to that gallery place about my pictures?'

'I did, and saw Mr Gish in person. He seemed intrigued.'

'Good.'

'I'm going to ring him up soon and ask how things are coming along.'

'Excellent. Keep after the blighter. If I can sell those pictures, I'll be able to live at Shipley again.'

'And I'll be able to marry Stanhope.'

'Ugh!'

'What did you say?'

'I didn't say anything.'

'You said "Ugh!"'

'Nothing of the kind.'

'It sounded like "Ugh!"'

'Very possibly. Many things do. But don't bother me now, my dear girl. I'm doing my crossword puzzle, and it's a stinker this morning. Run and ask Keggs what the dickens "Adventurer goes in for outrageous road-speed" is supposed to signify. Tell him it's urgent. And I want some more coffee.'

'You drink too much coffee.'

'Yer can't drink too much coffee. It bucks you up. It stimulates the mental processes.'

'All right, I'll get you some. What a lot of trouble you do give, to be sure.'

Jane returned with the coffee.

'I've made just one cup,' she said. 'I disapprove of you poisoning your system with caffeine. And that "road-speed" thing is an anagram, Mr Keggs says, and the answer is "desperado". Bung it down.'

'I will. Desperado, eh? Capital. Now, go and ask him what the devil "So the subordinate professional on trial gets wages in advance not without demur" means.'

'He's not here.'

'Don't be an ass. Of course he's here. He lives here, doesn't he?'

'He does. But at the moment he's off somewhere in his little car, going in for outrageous road-speed. I caught him just as he was leaving. Adieu, he cried, and waved his lily hand, and then he shot out into Mulberry Grove and headed for the great open spaces. You'll have to wait till he gets back,' said Jane, and went about her domestic duties. And Lord Uffenham, returning to his crossword puzzle, was wondering what sort of mind a man could have who was capable of springing a thing like 'So the subordinate professional on trial gets wages in advance not without demur' on a sensitive public, when from the corner of his eye he observed Stanhope Twine coming out of the back door of Peacehaven, his intention apparently to take a refreshing look at his masterpiece.

He rose in a marked manner and went into the house. He was in no mood to have 'Ah, Uffenham' said to him.

CHAPTER 4

At about the moment when Lord Uffenham was downing his first forkful of scrambled egg and the dog George the first of his two biscuits, the Roscoe Bunyan whom Jane Benedick disliked so much was standing beside his Jaguar outside a studio in St John's Wood, preparing to drive back to Shipley Hall and get some sleep. The party which he had gone up to London to attend had been one of those bohemian parties which last all night, terminating in a flurry of eggs and bacon as the postman is making his first delivery of the morning.

There was rather a lot of Roscoe Bunyan. As a boy, he had been a large, stout boy, inclined to hot dogs, candy and ice-cream sodas between meals, and he was no fonder of diet systems now than he had been in his formative years. Most of his acquaintances would have preferred far less of this singularly unattractive young man, but he had insisted on giving full measure, bulging freely in all directions. His face was red, the back of his neck overflowed his collar, and there had recently been published a second edition of his chin. It is not surprising, therefore, that such passers-by as had a love for the beautiful should have removed their gaze from him after a brief glance and transferred it to the girl who was standing beside him.

Elaine Dawn unquestionably took the eye. Nobody, looking at

her, would have supposed her to be the daughter of a Shoreditch public-house proprietor who had formerly been a heavyweight boxer. It often happens that fathers, incapable themselves of finishing in the first three in a seaside beauty contest, produce offspring who set the populace whistling, and this had occurred in the case of Elaine's parent, Battling Billson. He himself, partly because Nature had fashioned him that way and partly as the result of the risks of his profession, looked like a gorilla which had been caught in machinery of some sort, but this child was a breath-taking brunette of the Cleopatra type. One felt that she would have got on well with Mark Antony. Eyeing her as she stood here, Roscoe could understand why he had made that impulsive proposal of marriage in the later stages of another of those all-night parties two weeks before. She had what it takes to unsettle the cool judgment of the most level-headed young man.

The engagement had not been announced. Roscoe in an expansive moment had mentioned it to his guest Mortimer Bayliss, but Elaine had maintained a discreet silence about it. She thought it better so. A girl with parents like hers does not want those parents coming round to say Hello to their future son-in-law till it is too late for that son-in-law to realize the sort of family he is marrying into. Emma Billson loved and respected her father and mother, but she was a sensible girl, prudent and practical, and none realized more clearly than she that they were not everybody's money. Roscoe, some instinct told her, would not find them an encouraging spectacle. Time enough to confront him with them on the return from the honeymoon.

'Well,' said Roscoe, yawning cavernously, 'I'm off to grab some sleep. You'll get home all right?'

Miss Dawn lived out Pinner way, which is distant several miles from St John's Wood, and in a direction diametrically opposite to Shipley Hall. It speaks well for Roscoe's sturdy good sense that the idea of driving her there had never occurred to him. He, like his betrothed, was prudent and practical.

'Take a cab or something,' he said helpfully, and climbed into his Jaguar and was gone.

It was an hour and a quarter's drive from London to Shipley Hall, but Roscoe, who from earliest youth had been the sort of charioteer of whom traffic policemen inquire the locality of the fire, did it in forty-six minutes. Arriving and passing drowsily up the stairs to his bedroom, he was intercepted by Skidmore.

'Excuse me, sir,' said Skidmore. 'A Mr Keggs has called.'

Roscoe frowned.

'Keggs? I don't know any Keggs.'

'He tells me that he at one time held the post of butler to your father, sir.'

'Oh, that guy?' Out of the dead past there emerged slowly before Roscoe's mental eye a moon-faced figure with an Oxford accent and a spreading waistline. 'What does he want?'

'He did not say, sir, except to urge that the matter was important.'

'Where is he?'

'In my pantry, sir.'

Roscoe mused. Important? To whom? Oh, well, better see the man, perhaps, and get it over.

'All right, bring him into the smoking-room,' he said, and presently Keggs entered, bearing the bowler hat without which no butler, however ex, ever stirs abroad.

'Good morning, sir,' he said. 'I trust that you remember me, sir? I had the honour to serve the late Mr Bunyan senior many years ago in the capacity of butler.' His gooseberry eyes roamed to and fro, and he wheezed sentimentally for a moment. 'It seems strange to be in this room once more,' he observed genially. 'After returning from America, I was for some time in the service of Lord Uffenham at Shipley Hall. Revisiting it brings tears to my eyes.'

Roscoe was not interested in Keggs's eyes, though inclined, for he was of an impatient spirit and needed his sleep, to damn them.

'Get on,' he said curtly. 'What do you want?'

Keggs was silent for a moment, seeming to be marshalling his thoughts with a view to selecting the right opening. He looked at the bowler hat, and appeared to draw inspiration from it.

'You are a rich man, Mr Bunyan,' he began, and Roscoe started as though the Shipley Hall ghost had confronted him.

A faint, indulgent smile flitted for an instant across Keggs's face. He had interpreted that start.

'No, sir,' he went on. 'I have not come to borrow money. I was about to say that, though a rich man, you have probably no objection to becoming richer. Coming without further preamble to what I may call the *res*, sir, I am in a position to put you in the way of obtaining a million dollars.'

'What!'

'I speak in rough figures, of course. But I think it may be estimated at a million.'

It had frequently been said of Roscoe Bunyan by those who knew him that, though loaded down above the Plimsoll line with money, he would at no time refrain from walking ten miles in tight shoes to pick up a penny someone had dropped. He loved money as dearly as he loved food. When, therefore, retired butlers announced that they could put him in the way of obtaining a million dollars, they touched the deeps in him, and his whole soul, such as it was, became electrified. He stared at this bowler-hatted Santa Claus in much the same way as on another occasion stout

Cortez – though some say stout Balboa – stared at the Pacific. The suspicion that stout Keggs might be inebriated he dismissed instantly. The man's whole aspect radiated sobriety.

A sudden displeasing thought struck him. It was that his visitor was going to try to get him to put up money for something. He had some invention, possibly a patent corkscrew, for which he required financial backing, or, still worse, had in his possession the map, yellowed by the years, which showed – spot marked X – where Captain Kidd had buried his treasure. He snorted slightly, feeling that any such project must be nipped in the bud.

Keggs was just as good at interpreting snorts as at probing the inner meaning of starts. He raised a paternal hand, looking like a high priest rebuking an inferior priest for some lapse from the priestly standard.

'I think I divine what you have in mind, sir. You are under the impression that I wish you to finance a commercial venture of some nature.'

'Don't you?'

'No, sir. I have only information to sell.'

'Sell?' It was a verb that grated on Roscoe.

'Naturally I am desirous of receiving a certain emolument in return for my information.'

Roscoe chewed a dubious lip. He hated giving other people emoluments. All his life the money in his purse had been earmarked for the exclusive use of R. Bunyan. Still, if it was really true about that million dollars. . . .

'Well, all right. Shoot.'

'Very good, sir. I must begin,' said Keggs in a professional manner, 'by asking if the name of Tonti is familiar to you?'

'Never heard of him. Who is he?'

' "Was", sir, not "is". Tonti is no longer with us,' said Keggs, as who should say that all flesh is grass. 'He was an Italian banker who flourished in the seventeenth century, and originated what is known as the tontine, the nature of which I will explain. And now,' he concluded, having done so, 'if I may have your attention, sir, I will relate a brief story.'

He consulted the bowler hat again, and began.

'On the tenth of September, 1929, sir, your late father entertained at dinner at our Park Avenue residence eleven guests, all, with the exception of Mr Mortimer Bayliss, well-known financiers like himself. This, I need not remind you, was some weeks before the disastrous financial crash of the year 1929 occurred, and what is termed the bull market was at its height. All the gentlemen present had made and were making very large fortunes, and at the conclusion of the meal there was an exchange of views as to what should be done with all the money that was accruing daily in that era of frenzied speculation.'

Here Keggs, whom the passage of the years had left a little touched in the wind, paused for breath, and Roscoe took advantage of the momentary silence to ask him if he could not for God's sake speed it up a little. Would it not be possible for him, inquired Roscoe, to put a stick of dynamite under himself and come to the point?

'I was about to do so, sir,' said Keggs equably. 'The gentlemen, as I say, were discussing what would be the most amusing way of spending their money, and Mr Mortimer Bayliss, always fertile with suggestions, proposed a tontine. But a tontine differing from the one I was describing to you a moment ago. The idea of the scheme as originated by Tonti – of death gradually elminating all the competitors but one – made no appeal to the gentlemen, most of whom suffered from high blood-pressure, and it was then that Mr Bayliss offered this alternative proposal. It was, in a word, that Mr Bunyan and each of his guests should contribute fifty thousand dollars to a fund or pool, and that the entire sum – with compound interest over the years – should be paid to whichever of the contributors' sons was the last to become married. You spoke, sir?'

Roscoe had not spoken, he had snorted. But the snort he snorted now was a very different snort from the snort he had snorted when snorting previously. Then he had been cold and on his guard, alert to nip in the bud anything that could be classed under the heading of funny business or rannygazoo. Now he was eager, ardent, enthusiastic, and he expressed his emotion in an awestruck 'Gosh!'.

'The last to get married?'

'Yes, sir.'

'*I'm* not married.'

'No, sir.'

Golden visions rose before Roscoe's eyes.

'You're sure my father was in this?'

'Yes, sir.'

'He never said a word to me about it.'

'Secrecy and silence were of the essence, sir.'

'And this was in 1929?'

'Yes, sir.'

'Then—'

'Precisely, sir. In the course of the past twenty-five years the field, if I may employ a sporting expression, has thinned out. Several of the young gentlemen were eliminated in the recent global hostilities, while others have married. My *Times* informs me that Mr James Brewster, son of the late Mr John Brewster, became married yesterday. Until then he, yourself and one other gentleman were the sole survivors, as one might describe them.'

'You mean now there are only two of us?'

'Exactly, sir, only yourself and this other contestant. Who' – here Keggs paused significantly – 'is affianced—'

'Gosh!'

'And—' Keggs paused again. '– of straitened means.'

The glow which had warmed Roscoe at the word 'affianced' faded.

'Then he isn't likely to get married,' he said morosely. 'Dam it, he may not marry for years.'

Keggs coughed.

'Unless encouraged to do so by a little financial assistance from somebody more happily situated. As it might be yourself, sir.'

'Eh?'

'If you were to give the young gentleman financial assistance, it would quite possibly turn the scale. He would feel emboldened to take the plunge. Leaving you in possession of what, if you will pardon the argot, I might term the jackpot.'

Roscoe plucked at his double chin, debating within himself what to do for the best. And as he sat there at a young man's crossroads, Mortimer Bayliss sauntered in.

The years, which had dealt so gently with Augustus Keggs, had been rougher with Mortimer Bayliss, withering him till he now resembled something excavated from the tomb of one of the earlier Ptolemies. Seeing the visitor, he halted, raking him with the black-rimmed monocle which the passage of time had not succeeded in dislodging from his eye.

'Keggs!' he cried, astounded.

'Good morning, Mr Bayliss.'

'Aren't you dead yet? I thought we'd seen the last of you years ago. You're fatter than ever, my obese butler. *And* uglier. What on earth are you doing here?'

'I came to see Mr Bunyan on a matter of business, sir.'

'Oh, you're talking business? Then I'll leave you.'

'You won't!' said Roscoe, starting into life. 'You're just the man I want. Is it true what Keggs has been telling me?'

'Mr Bunyan is alluding to my account of what occurred at his father's dinner-table on the night of September the tenth, 1929, Mr Bayliss. Your suggestion of the matrimonial tontine, sir.'

It was not easy to disconcert Mortimer Bayliss, but at these words the monocle fell from his eye, and he stared incredulously.

'You know about that? For heaven's sake! Where were you? Under the table? Lurking in a corner, disguised as a potted palm?'

'No, sir, I was not present, except in spirit. But I had made a daily practice, from the very early beginnings of the bull market, of concealing a dictaphone behind the portrait of George Washington over the mantelpiece in the dining-room. I thought it might prove helpful to me in making my investments.'

'You mean you got a recording of every word spoken at those dinners of J. J.'s? You must have collected some pretty good market tips.'

'I did, sir. But none more profitable than yours, of selling my holdings and investing my money in government bonds.'

'You had the sense to do that?'

'I sold out next day, sir. I have always felt extremely grateful to you, Mr Bayliss. I look upon you as the founder of my fortunes.'

Roscoe, who had been listening with mounting impatience to these amiable exchanges, broke in on them petulantly.

'Never mind all that. To hell with your fortunes. Is it true about this tontine thing, Bayliss?'

'Quite true. It was one of my brightest ideas.'

'There really is this money coming to the son who's the last to marry?'

'Yes, it's all there, waiting.'

'And it works out at a million?'

'About that, I should imagine, by this time. Half a million was the original sum put up. One of the eleven—'

'Twelve.'

'Eleven, fool. You don't suppose a sonless bachelor like myself was going to contribute, do you? There was J. J., and there were ten of his guests, making eleven in all. And as I was about to tell you when you interrupted me with your fatuous remark, one of that eleven changed his mind in the calmer atmosphere of the morning after, and backed out. So there were ten starters at fifty thousand a head.'

'And only two of us left in now, Keggs says.'

'Indeed? I hadn't been following the race. Who's the other fellow?'

'I don't know yet.'

'And when you do know?'

'I'm going to fix him.'

'In what sense do you use the word fix?'

'Keggs says he wants to get married, but can't afford to. So I slip him something—'

'– and push him over the edge. I follow the train of thought. Nobbling the other horse. A thoroughly dirty trick. Whose idea was that?'

'Keggs's.'

'Oh? Well, you might not think it to look at me, Keggs, but I am blushing for you. Between the two of you, you seem to have turned what started out as a nice clean sporting contest into the lowest kind of ramp. And how about the wages of sin? I take it that Keggs expects a return of some sort for his skulduggery. What are you going to give him?'

Roscoe reflected for a moment.

'Fifty pounds,' he said, and Keggs, who had been fondling the bowler hat, started as if it had bitten him.

'Fifty pounds, sir?'

'What's wrong with fifty pounds?'

'I had expected rather more, sir.'

'You won't get it,' said Roscoe.

There was a silence. It was plain that Keggs had been cut to the quick and that the dream castles he had been building were shattered and lying about him in ruins. A butler never displays emotion, but he was an ex-butler, and he displayed quite a good deal. But presently the tempest within him became stilled. Calm returned to his moon-like features.

'Very good, sir,' he said, showing himself one of those stout-hearted men who can meet with triumph and disaster and treat those two impostors just the same, as recommended by Mr Kipling.

'Right,' said Mortimer Bayliss. 'So we can get on with it. Who is the mysterious unknown?'

'The name is Twine, sir.'

'Twine?' Roscoe turned to Mr Bayliss. 'I don't remember a friend of my father's called Twine. Do you?'

Mortimer Bayliss shrugged his shoulders.

'Why should I? Are you under the impression that the late J. J.'s loathsome associates were as a string of pearls to me and that I used to count them over, every one apart, my rosary, my rosary? Tell us about this Twine, Keggs.'

'He is a sculptor, sir. He resides next door to me.'

'Odd coincidence.'

'Yes, sir. It is a small world, I often say.'

'And who is he engaged to?'

'A Miss Benedick, sir, niece of the Lord Uffenham in whose service I was at one time. The young lady and his lordship reside at Castlewood.'

'Eh?'

'My house, sir. The address is Castlewood, Mulberry Grove, Valley Fields. Mr Twine is at Peacehaven.'

'Where he sculpts?'

'Yes, sir.'

'But not with great success, I gather?'

'No, sir. I should describe Mr Twine as fiscally crippled. This constitutes an obstacle in the way of his becoming united to the young lady.'

'Poverty is the banana skin on the doorstep of romance.'

'Precisely, sir.'

'And you suggest that Mr Bunyan should correct this state of things?'

'Yes, sir. I feel sure that Mr Twine would embark on matrimony immediately, if Mr Bunyan were to give him twenty thousand pounds.'

Roscoe quivered from stem to stern, his eyes popping from their sockets.

'Are you crazy?' he gasped. 'Twenty thousand pounds?'

'Sprat to catch a whale,' said Mortimer Bayliss. 'Don't spoil the ship for a ha'porth of tar, or, putting it another way, if you don't speculate, you can't accumulate.'

Roscoe ran a hand feverishly through his hair. Though he could see that there was sense in these platitudes, nothing was going to make them attractive to him.

'But how could I do it? You can't walk in on a man you've never met and give him money.'

'No, that's true. Any suggestions, Keggs?'

'It could be very simply arranged, sir. There is a statue of Mr Twine's in the garden of Peacehaven. A day or two ago, if I might suggest it, Mr Bunyan, calling on his father's former butler to talk of old times, happened to glance over the fence—'

'— and saw the masterpiece and was struck all of a heap? Of course. How right you are. You get the idea, Roscoe? "Egad!" you said, addressing yourself. "An undiscovered genius." And you decided to pop in on him with your cheque book.'

'And offer him twenty thousand pounds for a statue? He'll think I'm dippy.'

'How do you get around that, Keggs?'

'Quite easily, sir. I was perusing not long ago the auto-biography of an eminent playwright, in which he relates how, when merely a young man of promise, he was approached by a financial gentleman who offered him an annual income for a number of years in return for one-third of his, the playwright's, future earnings.'

'Did he accept it?'

'No, sir, but I am sure that Mr Twine would accept a similar offer from Mr Bunyan.'

'Of course he would, especially if the offer was twenty thousand pounds cash down. You can't miss, Roscoe. He'll start getting measured for the wedding trousers five minutes after he banks the cheque. And I'll tell you what I'll do. I'll handle the whole business for you. You need not appear except as a benevolent figure in the background. What's this Twine's telephone number, Keggs? I'll go and talk to him now.'

Some minutes had passed before he returned, minutes occupied by Roscoe in gazing bleakly into space, by Keggs in fondling the bowler hat. A tentative remark by the ex-butler dealing with the continued fineness of the June weather was poorly received. Roscoe was not in a conversational mood.

'I've talked to him,' said Mortimer Bayliss, 'and his reception of my name was, I must say, extremely gratifying. "Not *the* Mortimer Bayliss?" he gurgled. "None other," I replied, blushing prettily. And then I told him how you had seen the statue and been greatly impressed by it and wanted me to give my expert opinion of it and his other works, which are probably too foul for words, eh, Keggs?'

'I do not admire them myself, sir.'

'And the upshot of it all is that he has invited me to dinner tonight at Wee Holme. Or is it Kosy-Kot?'

'Peacehaven, sir.'

'Just as bad, if not worse. I suppose I shall get the usual loathsome suburban dinner.'

'No, sir. Mr Twine has an excellent cook.'

'He has? Well, that's something. It will help me to endure what will undoubtedly be a ghastly evening, for if there is one thing I hate, it is busts in any quantity. J. J. was always trying to make me buy him busts. He had a morbid passion for them. So much, then, for this evening. Tomorrow I shall allow him to simmer and the day after give him lunch at my club and spring the proposition on him. I had better take your cheque with me, so that I can flutter it before his eyes. And you ought to thank Keggs for his shrewd suggestion.'

Roscoe gulped. He was suffering as only a parsimonious multi-millionaire can suffer when faced with the prospect of becoming separated from twenty thousand pounds. But he could see that

the investment was a sound one. A sprat, as Mortimer Bayliss
had said, to catch a whale. Nevertheless, as he spoke, his voice
was hollow.

'Thank you, Keggs.'

'Not at all, sir. A pleasure. Good morning, sir. Good morning,
Mr Bayliss.'

'You leaving us?'

'I ought to be getting back, sir.'

'Train?'

'I have my car.'

'I'll see you to it. Keggs,' said Mortimer Bayliss, closing the
door behind them and halting before him with monocle poised
and a look on his mummified face like that of a district attorney
about to cross-examine the stuffing out of a rat of the underworld, 'A word with you, my fishy major-domo. What's the
game?'

'Sir?'

'Wipe that blasted saintly expression off your fat face, moron.
What, I asked, is the game, and I should like a categorical answer.
Come clean, you bowler-hatted hellhound. You know as well as
I do that J. J. Bunyan never had a friend called Twine.'

It would be too much to say that Keggs giggled. Butlers, even
when retired, do not giggle. But he came very near to giggling.

'I was asking myself if that point had struck you, sir.'

'Well, tell yourself it did.'

'I feared for a moment that you were about to expose my little
deception.'

Mortimer Bayliss raised his eyebrows.

'My good Keggs, when I see a situation developing which
promises to culminate in Roscoe Bunyan paying out twenty
thousand pounds for nothing, I allow it to develop. I don't spoil

the fun by exposing little deceptions. Heaven knows there aren't too many chances of getting a good laugh these days.'

'No, indeed, sir.'

'A benevolent Providence has been saving up something like this for Roscoe for years. He's far too fond of money. Very bad for his soul. It is doing him a kindness to take some of it off him from time to time. You felt that, eh?'

'Very strongly, sir.'

'Yes, I could see you feeling it when he spoke of rewarding you for your services with fifty pounds in full settlement.'

'The offer did seem to me in the circumstances somewhat inadequate, I confess.'

'So you gave him what is called the wrong steer by way of getting back at him?'

'I was also actuated by a genuine desire to be of service to Miss Benedick, sir. A charming young lady. I would not say that I consider Mr Twine an ideal mate for Miss Benedick, but she appears to be in favour of the union, so I am only too happy to be instrumental in bringing it to fruition.'

'Golly!'

'Sir?'

'Nothing. I was only admiring the way you talk. Has anyone ever called you the Boy Orator of Valley Fields?'

'Not to my knowledge, sir.'

'Posterity will. And now, my dear Keggs, tell me – briefly, if you can manage it – who is the real McCoy?'

'Sir?'

'The genuine one, fathead. The true claimant, ass. Roscoe's rival.'

'Oh, I beg your pardon, sir. You misled me for a moment by alluding to him as McCoy. His name is Hollister.'

'What!' The information seemed to surprise Mortimer Bay-liss. 'You mean Joe Hollister's son?'

'I believe Mr Hollister senior's name was Joseph.'

'I know darned well it was. He was my best – I might say my only – friend. Why, it is impossible to say, but I have never been a popular man. What's young Bill Hollister doing these days? The last I heard of him, he was going to learn painting . . . in Paris.'

'Mr Hollister junior is at present employed as an assistant at the well-known Gish Galleries in Bond Street.'

'That den of thieves! And he's engaged to be married, you say?'

'To a Miss Angela Murphrey, sir, a lady who studies the violin at the Royal College of Music.'

'How the devil do you know all this?'

'Through the good offices of the investigation bureau which I have been employing, sir.'

'Good God! You put a private eye on to him?'

'It was the simplest method of keeping myself *au courant* with his affairs.'

'God bless you, Keggs! You ought to be head of the secret police in Moscow.'

'I doubt if I would care for residence in Russia, sir. The climate. Would there be anything further, Mr Bayliss?'

'No, I think that about winds up the agenda. God bless you again, my Keggs, making twice in all.'

Mortimer Bayliss went back to Roscoe. A more cheerful Roscoe now, for he had been thinking things over and had adjusted himself to the high cost of sprats.

'Keggs gone?' he said.

'Yes, he has departed, and in what looked to me like dudgeon. Fifty pounds, Roscoe! Not much of a tip, considering everything. Have you no regrets?'

'Of course I haven't.'

'You may ere long.'

'What do you mean?'

'Oh, nothing. You know,' said Mortimer Bayliss, 'there's one thing about this business that you appear to have overlooked.'

'Eh?'

'How about your own wedding? I seem to remember you telling me you were engaged.'

'Oh, that? I'll break it off, of course.'

'I see. Break it off. And what about breach of promise actions? I suppose you've written her letters?'

'One or two.'

'Mentioning marriage?'

'Yes, I did mention marriage.'

'Then you'd better start worrying.'

'No need to worry. It's all right.'

'Why – I am a child in these matters – is it all right?'

'I know an excellent man called Pilbeam, who runs the Argus Inquiry Agency— He'll get those letters for me. I gave him the same sort of job about a year ago, and he did it without a hitch. He's always doing that sort of thing. Of course, I won't break off the engagement till I've got them.'

Mortimer Bayliss threw his head back, and the room rang with the cackling laughter which twenty-six years ago had too often rasped the nerves of J. J. Bunyan's guests.

'The last of the Romantics! What a rare soul you are, Roscoe. You remind me of Sir Galahad.'

CHAPTER 5

The sun was high in the sky above London's West End and all good men had long since buckled down to the day's work at their shops and offices, when a young man with a headache turned out of Piccadilly and started to walk up Bond Street, a square-jawed, solidly built young man who looked less like the art-gallery assistant he actually was than a contender for the middleweight championship who has broken training for a while. His name was Bill Hollister, and the headache from which he was suffering was due to the fact that he, like Roscoe Bunyan, had been one of the revellers at that all-night party at the St John's Wood studio.

But though an unseen hand had begun at brief intervals to drive red-hot spikes rather briskly through his temples, his heart was light and he was in two minds about whistling a gay tune. Like the heroine of the poet Browning's *Pippa Passes*, he was of the opinion that God was in His heaven and all right with the world. Indeed, if Pippa had happened to pass at that moment, he would have slapped her on the back and told her he knew just how she felt.

It has been well said – among others by Lord Uffenham, who in his salad days was always having trouble through getting engaged to the wrong girl – that there is no ecstasy so profound as that which comes to a young man who is unexpectedly given his freedom by a fiancée for whom he has never much cared, to whom he proposed in what, he feels, must have been one of those moments of madness, sheer madness, which people are always having on radio and in television. And this had happened to Bill. Uneasily betrothed for the past month to the Miss Angela Murphrey of whom Keggs had spoken to Mortimer Bayliss, he had found awaiting him on his return from the St John's Wood party a letter from her, formally severing their relations, and it had acted on him like benzedrine.

It had not come wholly as a surprise, this letter, for Miss Murphrey had for some little time been throwing out hints that suggested that she might be dubious as to his suitability as a life partner. She was one of those forceful girls who do not shrink from speaking their minds when they detect flaws in their chosen mates. 'Why don't you brush your hair?' she would say to her William. 'You look like a sheep dog.' Or, again, 'Why do you wear that awful cutaway coat and those striped trousers? You look like an undertaker.' Useless to tell her that the cross he had to bear was that every time he brushed his hair it sprang out of shape again the moment the brush was removed. Equally useless to plead that he was compelled to wear a cutaway coat and striped trousers because they were the uniform of his guild, and to explain that if an assistant of his were to show up at the Gish Galleries in mufti, Mr Gish would have him shot at sunrise. A melancholy silence was his only course.

Coming right down to it, then, practically all Bill Hollister had got out of his association with Miss Murphrey was the discovery that his personal appearance was that of a shaggy dog, expert at herding sheep, which had taken up mortician work in its spare time, and surely, he felt, a marriage of true minds should have produced something a little warmer. The thought that from now on Miss Murphrey would take the high road while he took the low road, and that neither on the bonnie bonnie banks of Loch Lomond nor elsewhere would they ever meet again, was a very stimulating one. An assistant who worked at the Gish Galleries was supposed to be at his post by nine-thirty, but though the hour was now eleven forty-five and he knew that behind those portals Leonard Gish must be crouching to spring, a Leonard Gish whose bite might well be fatal, he refused to allow the shape of things to come to diminish his feeling of *bien-être*. Arriving at his destination, he beamed on the young woman who sat in the outer office, a Miss Elphinstone, and greeted her exuberantly, as one who after much searching has found an old friend.

'Good morning, Elphinstone, good morning, good morning, good morning. Everything under control?'

In Miss Elphinstone's gaze there was no answering exuberance, only austere rebuke and a chilly disapproval. There had always been something Murphreyesque about this lady receptionist, as she liked to describe herself, and many a time had Bill urged her to take the lemon out of her mouth and look on the bright side, stressing the fact that the world was so full of a number of things that he was sure we should all be as happy as kings.

'Ho!' she said.

'Ho to you,' responded Bill civilly.

'Well, if I'd known you were coming, I'd have baked a cake,' said Miss Elphinstone. 'This is a nice time to be starting work.'

'I would prefer not to hear that word "work" mentioned,' said Bill with a touch of stiffness. 'It does something to me this morning.'

'Coming here at twelve o'clock.'

'Ah, now I get you. A little late, you feel? Yes, possibly you're right. I was at a party last night and got home with the milk. A photo finish. Sinking into a chair, I dozed off, and who more surprised than I to find on waking that it was past eleven. Elphinstone,' said Bill, eyeing her closely, 'I don't like that yellow make-up you're using this morning. And why do you flicker at the rims? It's a most disturbing spectacle.'

'You'll flicker when Mr Gish sees you. He's been jumping around like a cat on a hot shovel.'

'You probably mean a pea in that painful position, but I take your point. Cross, is he? I'm sorry to hear that, for this morning I want to have smiling faces about me. You see me today, Elphinstone, sitting on top of the world with a rainbow round my shoulder and my hat on the side of my head. You don't understand why, not knowing the facts, but I feel like a caged skylark that has been freed and permitted to soar into the empyrean with a song on its lips. If Shelley were to see me now, he would say "Hail to thee, blithe spirit", and he would mean it. I feel . . . but as something in your manner tells me that you don't give a hoot how I feel, and as Pop Gish no doubt wishes to have speech with me, I will be getting in touch with him.'

'He's gone.'

'Already? Before lunch?'

'He's gone to the country to the sale of some old furniture.'

'Oh, I see.' The stern look faded from Bill's face. 'I feared for a moment that he had turned into a clock-watcher and was not giving his all to the dear old gallery. Well, if you had mentioned this sooner, I would have been spared considerable nervous tension. I was picturing him in there all ready to attack me with tooth and claw. Did the fine old man leave any little messages for me?'

'He said tell you that if you want to jump into the river with a pound of lead in each hand, it will be all right with him.'

'That was not the true Leonard Gish speaking. He will be sorry for those harsh words later on, when he has had time to reflect. Any further instructions? Remember that my motto is Service.'

'Yes, there was something about some pictures at some house down in Kent. You'll find the address on his desk. He wants you to go and look at them this afternoon.'

'No,' said Bill. Here he felt he had to be firm. 'I'll do anything in reason, but I won't go anywhere this afternoon. Make it tomorrow.'

'Suit yourself. It's no skin off *my* nose.'

'What deplorably vulgar expressions you use, Elphinstone. I sometimes feel all the trouble I have taken to educate you has been thrown away. Very disheartening. And stop *flickering*, woman. I've had to speak to you about this before. Anything else?'

'Yes, he said ... wait a minute, he wrote it down ... He said if Mrs Weston-Smythe comes in, you're to show her first the "Follower of El Greco", then the "Diaz Flower Piece", then the "Pupil of the Master of the Holy Kinship of Cologne", and then the "Bernardo Daddi".'

'My heart belongs to Daddi.'

'And be sure to get them in the right order. Does that mean anything to you?'

'Clear as mud. It is what is known as easing the sucker into it. It's like when you tell a story that's leading up to a smashing finish and make the early stages of it as dull as possible so as to heighten the effect of the final snapperoo. The one we want to sell her is the Daddi, so we pave the way with the follower and the flower piece and the pupil, each lousier than the last.

These you might describe as the come-ons. They are designed to lower the spirits of Mrs Weston-Smythe and make her feel that this is what she gets for belonging to the human race. Then, while she is still wallowing in the depths, wondering what she can do to shake off this awful depression, we flash the Daddi at her. Naturally, after all that build-up, it looks to her like the picture of her dreams, and she buys it. Psychological stuff.'

Miss Elphinstone regarded him with a novel respect.

'I call that clever. I had no idea you really knew anything about this business. I thought you were—'

'Just one of the sheep dogs? Far, far from it. My diffident manner misleads people. Anything else?'

'Oh, yes. There was someone on the 'phone for you just now. Spine, he said his name was.'

'Not Spine. Twine. A club acquaintance, and between ourselves something of a pill. What did he want?'

'How should I know?'

'Well, I'm glad I didn't have to talk to him, for I am in no condition for telephone conversations as of even date. It's curious, the way I'm feeling this morning. Spiritually, I am right up there with the Cherubim and Seraphim and likely at any moment to start singing Hosanna, but physically you see me not at my superb best. My head aches and a drowsy numbness pains my sense, as though of hemlock I had drunk or emptied some dull opiate to the drains one minute past and Lethe-wards had sunk. Keats had the same experience. You are a young girl starting out in life, Elphinstone, so I'll give you a word of advice which will be useful to you. Stay away from bohemian revels in artists' studios. And if you feel you must go in for bohemian revels, insist on being served barley water. Only so in the cold grey light of the morning after will you escape having a head that feels as if it had been blown up with a bicycle pump to approximately three times its proper-size?'

It was some minutes later, as Bill was resting the head of which he had spoken against the telephone in the hope of cooling it, that the instrument suddenly jerked him out of his repose by ringing. Wearily lifting the receiver, he found his ear assaulted by a high-pitched voice.

'Hullo,' it said. 'Hullo. Are you there?'

'No,' said Bill, 'I'm not. Go away.'

'Is that you, Hollister? This is Twine. Listen, Hollister, didn't you tell me once that you knew Mortimer Bayliss?'

'When I was a boy. He used to come and play chess with my father, and curse me for peering over his shoulder. Why?'

'I'm giving him dinner tonight.'

'Then you'd better make it a good one. Because he's extremely apt, if anything goes wrong with the catering, to stab you with a fish fork. A testy character, this Bayliss, a human snapping turtle. How did you get mixed up with him?'

'It's rather extraordinary. Do you know a man called Bunyan at the club?'

'Roscoe Bunyan? Land sakes, honeychile, I've known him since we were both so high. We were boys together. How does he come into it?'

'Apparently he's seen some of my things and liked them, and he's told Bayliss to look at them and give his opinion. So I asked him to dine tonight, and I was wondering if you would come along.'

'You want me to give you moral support?'

'Yes, I do. You know him, and you've got the gift of the gab.'

'I would prefer to be called an entertaining conversationalist.'

'You can talk to him at dinner. Then after dinner you just clear out and leave me to show him my things.'

'I see.'

'You will come, won't you?'

There was a pleading note in Stanhope Twine's voice, which it was not easy for one of Bill's amiability to resist. He was not particularly fond of Stanhope Twine, whom actually he knew only very slightly through meeting him occasionally at the club to which they both belonged, but he could appreciate that this was a big opportunity for him and it would, he felt, be churlish to withhold his aid in helping things along. There had always been something of the Boy Scout in Bill Hollister.

He was, moreover, looking forward to meeting Mortimer Bayliss again. He had described him to Stanhope Twine as a human snapping turtle, and a human snapping turtle, unless the years had mellowed him, turning him into a kindly old gentleman with a fondness for the society of his juniors, he no doubt still was. But Bill knew him to be one of those snapping turtles which beneath rough exteriors conceal hearts of gold. He had learned from his late father that, when the crash of 1929 had wiped out the Hollister fortune, it was Mortimer Bayliss who had come to the rescue, full of strange oaths but bearing a cheque book and fountain pen and offering to write a cheque for any amount his old friend might require to see him through the bad times. You might have to dig for the rich ore in Mortimer Bayliss, but it was there.

'All right,' he said. 'I was rather thinking of staying at home and quietly passing beyond the veil, but I'll be with you.'

'Good. Peacehaven, Mulberry Grove, Valley Fields, is the address. You know how to get to Valley Fields?'

'My native guide 'Mbongo will find the way. Most capable fellow.'

'Somewhere around seven.'

'Right.'

Bill replaced the receiver, and looked at his watch. Yes, as he had supposed, time for lunch. He found his hat, gave Miss Elphinstone a friendly pat on the back hair, and started out to see if he could toy with a little something.

CHAPTER 6

Preparations for Stanhope Twine's dinner party began immediately after Mortimer Bayliss had concluded his telephone call, and Mulberry Grove was astir. Stanhope Twine told the news to Jane over the fence, and Jane lost no time in seeking out her Uncle George, to inform him that he would have to take the evening meal elsewhere tonight. She found him in his study having difficulties with 'Tree gets mixed up with comic hat in scene of his triumphs', and for a while listened sympathetically while he spoke his mind on the subject of the smart alecks who compose crossword puzzles these days. Lord Uffenham had been brought up in the sound old tradition of the Sun God Ra and the large Australian bird Emu, and he resented all this new-fangled stuff about subordinate professionals and comic hats. It made him sick, he said, and Jane said she didn't wonder.

'And now touching on dinner tonight. Would you like caviar to start with, followed by clear soup, roast chicken with bread sauce and two veg, poires Hélène and a jam omelette?'

'Capital.'

'Well, you won't get them,' said Jane brutally. 'Tonight's the night of Stanhope's big dinner party, and I shall be over at Peace-haven, cooking for it. We're doing things in style, to impress Mr Bayliss.'

'Hey?'

'Mortimer Bayliss. Very celebrated old gentleman, I gather, and no fault of his that I've never heard of him in my life. Apparently he's something very big and important in the Art world, and he's coming to look at Stanhope's busts and things. I do hope he'll like Stanhope.'

'Did yer say like *Stanhope*?'

'I did.'

'I see. Puzzled me for a moment. However,' said Lord Uffenham, skillfully evading the danger point, 'that is neither here nor there. The point to keep the eye on is that there won't be any dinner for me. All right, I'll get a chop at the local. I'll take Keggs along.'

'You won't. Mr Keggs has promised to come out of his retirement and buttle. I told you we were doing things in style. We plan to knock this Bayliss's eye out.'

And so it came about that the first thing on which Bill Hollister's eye rested, when the front door of Peacehaven opened at seven o'clock that night, was Augustus Keggs, looking like something out of an Edwardian drawing-room comedy. The spectacle rocked him back on his heels. The last thing he had expected to encounter in this remote suburb was a vintage butler of obviously a very good year.

'Mr Twine?' he said, recovering.

'Mr Twine has had to step out to purchase cigarettes, sir. He will be returning shortly. If you would take a seat.'

Bill took a seat, but it was not long before the beauty of the evening drew him out into the garden. Like those of The Nook to the left and Castlewood to the right, it was on the small side, and its features of interest were soon exhausted. Having admired the summerhouse and the bird bath and winced away from the statue, he glanced over the right-hand fence in the hope of finding something more intriguing there, and was rewarded with the spectacle of a large, pear-shaped man of elderly aspect, who was digging in a flower bed with a spade.

Digging is strenuous work, and if you are past your first youth, you cannot do it for long without getting a crick in the back. Presently Lord Uffenham straightened himself and, seeing Bill, came lumbering toward him. He always welcomed the opportunity to exchange ideas with his fellow men.

'Nice evening,' he said.

'Very,' said Bill.

'Ever do crossword puzzles?'

'Sometimes.'

'Don't happen to know what the answer to "Tree gets mixed up with comic hat in scene of his triumphs" would be, do yer?'

'I'm afraid not.'

'Thought yer probably wouldn't. Well, what the hell? These bally crossword puzzles are just a waste of time. Forget the whole thing, I say.'

'The right spirit.'

'Life's too short.'

'Much too short,' agreed Bill.

Lord Uffenham removed a segment of soil from his jutting chin, and prepared to change the subject. Over his tea and buttered toast that afternoon he had read an item in the evening paper that had made a deep impression on him. He was always reading things in the papers that brought him up with a round turn.

'Hey!' he said.

'Yes?' said Bill.

'Tell yer something that'll surprise yer,' said Lord Uffenham. 'Know how many people are born every year?'

'Down here, do you mean?'

'No, all over the bally place. England, America, China, Japan, Africa, everywhere. Thirty-six million.'

'You don't say?'

'Fact. Every year there are thirty-six million more people in the world. Makes yer think a bit, that.'

'It does indeed.'

'Thirty-six million. And half of them probably sculptors. As if there weren't enough ruddy sculptors in the world already.'

'You don't like sculptors?'

'Scum of the earth.'

'Yet sculptors are also God's creatures.'

'In a sense, yerss. But they've no right to leave things like that lying about the place.'

Bill glanced at the colossal nude.

'It does take up space which might be utilized for other purposes,' he assented. 'But no doubt Twine admires it.'

'He a friend of yours?'

'We belong to the same club.'

'Must be an easy club to get into. What d'yer make the time?'

'Seven-twenty.'

'Late as that? I must be getting off to that chop.'

'What chop would that be?'

'I'm having dinner at the pub.'

'May good digestion wait on appetite.'

'Hey? Oh, Yerss. Yerss, I see what yer mean. Very well put. Good evening to yer, sir,' said Lord Uffenham, and lumbered off. And Bill, greatly uplifted, as anyone would have been, by these intellectual exchanges with what was evidently one of Valley Fields's best minds, was making his way to the house, when Mortimer Bayliss came out of it.

'Oh, hello, Mr Bayliss,' said Bill. 'You probably won't remember me. Bill Hollister.'

He was thinking, as he spoke, how incredibly ancient the other looked. But though he gave the impression that he would never see a hundred and four again, it was plain that there still lingered in the curator of the Bunyan Collection the fire which in the old days had caused him so seldom to be invited twice to the same house.

'Bill Hollister? Yes, I remember you. A loathsome little blot you were, too. You used to breathe down the back of my neck when I came to play chess with your father. An ugly ginger-headed brute of a boy with a revolting grin and, as far as I was able to ascertain, no redeeming qualities of any sort. Did you know that when you were born, it was only by maintaining an iron front that I avoided becoming your godfather? Phew! That was a narrow escape.'

A feeling of warm affection for Mortimer Bayliss had come over Bill.

'You missed a good thing,' he said. 'You might have been the envy of all. People are always coming up to me in the street and saying "I wish you were my godson". I've improved enormously since those early days.'

'Nonsense. I should say you were probably, if anything, more loathsome than ever. Extraordinary that you should have got any girl to look at you. Yet somebody told me you were engaged to be married.'

'Who?'

'Never you mind. I have my sources of information. Are you?'

'No longer.'

'Had the sense to get out of it, did you? Good. And I hear you work for old Gish.'

'Yes. If you ask him, he'll probably say I don't, but I do.'

'You didn't keep on with your painting, then?'

'I couldn't make a go of it.'

'Too good for the rabble?'

'That's what I've always thought.'

'And it suddenly struck you, I suppose, that you had to eat?'

'Exactly. And thanks to Gish this can be arranged. On a modest scale, of course, nothing elaborate. But how did you know I had ever tried to be a painter?'

'The last time I saw your father, a year or two before he died, he told me you were going to study in Paris,' said Mortimer Bayliss, omitting to mention that it was he who had given the late Mr Hollister the money to pay for Bill's studies. 'I had dreams of being a painter, myself at one time, but I woke up. Much simpler, I found, to tell other people how to paint.' He cocked his monocle at a willowy form that had emerged from the house and was hurrying down the garden path toward them. 'What bloody man is this?' he asked, becoming Shakespearian.

'That is our host, Stanhope Twine.'

'Looks a bit of a poop.'

'And is. Hello, Stanhope.'

Stanhope Twine was all high voice and agitation.

'Hullo, Hollister. I'm terribly, terribly sorry I wasn't here when you arrived, Mr Bayliss. I went out to get some cigarettes for you.'

'Never smoke the filthy things,' said Mortimer Bayliss cordially. 'And if you're going to offer me a cocktail, don't. I never touch them.'

'Do you drink sherry?'

'I don't drink anything. Gave it up years ago.'

'You do eat, don't you?' asked Bill with some concern. 'We want this thing to be a success.'

Mortimer Bayliss eyed him coldly.

'Are you being funny?'

'Trying to be.'

'Try harder,' Mortimer Bayliss advised.

'Dinner is served, sir,' said Keggs, materializing out of thin air at their side, as is the way with the best butlers. You think they aren't there, and then you suddenly find they are.

CHAPTER 7

Obedient to his host's instructions, Bill detached himself from the party reasonably soon after Keggs had served the coffee, and at nine-thirty was out in the garden again, reclining in a deck chair and gazing up at the stars.

It had been an unexpectedly enjoyable evening, for Mortimer Bayliss had tapped a vein of geniality of which his best friends – if any – would not have believed him capable. Softened by a superb dinner superbly served by a butler who had – no easy feat – in his day satisfied J. J. Bunyan, he conveyed the impression that a child could have played with him and, furthermore, that had such a child been present, he would have patted its head and given it sixpence. His table talk, with its flow of anecdote about shady millionaires and shadier Roumanian art dealers, had been gay and sparkling, and Bill would gladly have had more of it. But he could understand Stanhope Twine, the ice broken, wanting to have this mellowed and influential man to himself, so had withdrawn as per gentlemen's agreement.

The garden, which had been so pleasant at seven-twenty, was even pleasanter at half past nine, for it was wrapped now in the velvet stillness of the summer night. Though stillness is, of course, a relative term. Bill, relaxed in his chair, was in a position to hear a pianist, who appeared to be of tender years and to have learned his art through the medium of a correspondence course, playing what sounded like Tinkling Tunes For The Tots at The Nook next door and, further afield, the blare of the television set at Balmoral in the adjoining road, while at another house in the same neighbourhood – Chatsworth – somebody whose voice would have been the better for treatment with sandpaper was rendering extracts from the works of Gilbert and Sullivan.

Nevertheless, though he wished the Balmoral bunch would turn down that TV set a bit and the virtuoso at The Nook give up the unequal struggle and go to bed, he found Valley Fields by night very soothing, and quickly surrendered to its gentle magic. Like Major Flood-Smith, he had difficulty in believing that only a few miles separated him from the roar and bustle of the metropolis, and it is possible that he would shortly have fallen into a restful sleep, had not his attention at this moment been drawn to a singular – it would not be too much to say sinister – spectacle. On the lawn, only a few yards from where he sat, a light was flickering to and fro. Some creature of the night had invaded the privacy of Peacehaven with an electric torch.

When you are a man's guest, even if that man is one for whom you feel no great affection, you cannot ignore the presence in his garden of prowlers. His bread and salt have placed you under an obligation. Bill, obeying this unwritten law, rose noiselessly and advanced with stealth on the intruder, modelling his technique on that of those Fenimore Cooper Indians who were accustomed to move from spot to spot without letting a twig snap beneath their feet. Arriving behind a dark figure and feeling that he could not do better than borrow from the vocabulary of Miss Elphin-stone,' he said:

'Ho!'

and Lord Uffenham, for it was he, spun round with a loud snort.

It is always difficult to pin down to an exact point in time the birth of an inspiration, for one never knows how long it may not have been lurking unnoticed in the subconscious. Quite possibly the idea of climbing the fence into Stanhope Twine's garden, armed with a pot of black paint, and painting on the chin of his colossal nude a small imperial beard of the type worn by ambassadors had been burgeoning within Lord Uffenham for weeks. But it was only as he walked back from the Green Lion in Rosendale Road after his frugal dinner that the thought stole into the upper reaches of his mind that a small imperial beard was just what the colossal nude needed and that he would never have a better opportunity of applying it than now. His niece Jane was in the Peacehaven kitchen. Augustus Keggs was busy buttling. And Stanhope Twine and his guests were safely indoors. Conditions, in a word, could scarcely have been improved upon.

So reasoned Lord Uffenham, and it was consequently a most unpleasant shock to him when that 'Ho!' came at him out of the darkness, indicating that others beside himself were abroad in the night. To the fact that he would tomorrow be closely grilled by his niece he had steeled himself. A man with a mission can face these unpleasantnesses. But he had not bargained for fellow-travellers. Their presence disturbed him, especially when they said 'Ho!' like that. And now, adding to his discomfort, a clutching hand grasped his nose, twisting it in the manner of a hand that intended to stand no nonsense. The pain was considerable, and his agonized 'Hey!' nearly drowned the television set at Balmoral.

Anyone who had once heard Lord Uffenham say 'Hey!' was able ever afterwards to recognize its distinctive note, and Bill, it will be recalled, had enjoyed that experience. This, he realized, could be no other than his pre-dinner acquaintance who had spoken so searchingly of sculptors.

'Oh, it's you,' he said, releasing the nose, and there was a moment of silence. Then the wounded man spoke in a voice vibrant with feeling.

'If yer know me a thousand years,' he said, 'never do that again. I thought it was coming off at the roots.'

'I'm sorry.'

'No good being sorry now.'

'I took you for a midnight marauder.'

'How d'yer mean, midnight? It's only ten.'

'Well, a ten-o'clock marauder. It seemed odd that you should be prowling about Twine's garden with a flashlight.'

Lord Uffenham had recovered his poise. He was his old self again now, the fine sturdy old gentleman who had so often looked his niece Jane in the eye, stoutly denying all charges and generally managing to get away with it.

'Lord love a duck,' he said. 'Aren't you familiar with life in the suburbs?'

'Not very. I'm more the metropolitan type.'

'Well, we're like one great big family down here. I stroll in your garden, you stroll in mine. You borrow my roller, I borrow yours.'

'Wholesome give and take.'

'Exactly. Tomorrow in all probability I shall look out of the window and see Stanhope Twine on my lawn. "Ah, Twine", I shall say, and he will reply "Good morning, good morning". All very pleasant and neighbourly. Still, it might be as well if yer didn't mention to him that yer found me here. He's a little nervous just now about people coming into his garden, because he's afraid they may leave finger marks on that statue of his.

There are some children at The Nook next door, who occasionally pot at it with catapults, and this makes him sensitive. So just forget yer saw me.'

'I will.'

'Thank yer, my boy. I knew you'd understand. You're the feller I was talking to before dinner, aren't yer?'

'That's right. How was the chop?'

'What chop?'

'Your chop.'

'Oh, that chop? There wasn't any chop. Had to have liver and bacon.'

'Tough.'

'Yerss, it was, rather. But I can rough it. You been dining with Twine?'

'Yes.'

'How did yer get away?' asked Lord Uffenham, rather in the manner of a Parisian of pre-Revolutionary days addressing a friend who, when last heard of, had been in the Bastille.

'I was driven out into the snow. Twine wanted to be alone with his other guest, a man who is interested in his work.'

'Interested in Twine's work? He must be potty. Well,' said Lord Uffenham, suddenly realizing that time was flying and that his niece Jane would be heading for home ere long, 'can't stop here talking to you all night, much as I've enjoyed seeing yer again. If yer'll give me a hand over the fence, I think I'll be getting back.'

When Jane returned, he wanted her to find him in his study with a good book, curled up in an armchair and not having stirred from it for hours.

CHAPTER 8

The coming of a new day found George, sixth Viscount Uffenham, who on the previous night had sown the wind, reaping the whirlwind. One glance at his niece Jane as she entered the study where he sat trying to ascertain what the composer of his crossword puzzle meant by the words 'Spasmodic as a busy tailor', had been enough to tell his practised eye that she was ratty, hot under the collar and madder than a wet hen.

'Uncle George,' she said, and, musical though her voice was, Lord Uffenham did not like it. 'Was it you who painted that moustache on Stanhope's statue?'

It was most fortunate that she should have worded her inquiry thus, for it enabled Lord Uffenham to deny the accusation with a clear conscience. What he had painted on Stanhope Twine's statue, it will be recalled, was a small imperial beard.

'Certainly not,' he said with a dignity that became him well. 'Wouldn't dream of doing such a thing.'

'It must have been you.'

'Ridiculous.'

'Who else could it have been?'

'Hey?'

'It's no use pretending to go into one of your trances. You heard what I said.'

'Yerss, I heard what you said, and it shocked me. Let's get this thing straight. Someone, you say, has been painting a moustache on that Ladies Night In a Turkish Bath eyesore of Twine's. Well and good. Just what it needed. But if you think it was me—'

'I do.'

'Then ask yerself one question.'

'What question?'

'I'll tell yer what question. Ask yerself if it's likely that a busy man like me, a man with a hundred calls on his time, would go about the place painting moustaches on statues. Lord love a duck, you'll be saying next . . . I don't know what you'll be saying next,' said Lord Uffenham, frankly giving the thing up. 'Changing the subject, it says here in my crossword puzzle "Spasmodic as a busy tailor", and if yer can tell me what the hell that means—'

'I don't propose to change the subject.'

'Oh, all right, let's go on threshing it out, though I doubt if we'll get anywhere. Waste of time, if yer ask me. How's Twine? Is he ratty?'

'He's furious,' said Jane, and was conscious of a slight discomfort as she remembered how shrill her betrothed had become in his hour of travail. Stanhope Twine was one of those men who are not at their best when upset.

'Well, it's no good him trying to fasten it on me. The charge won't stick. It was probably one of those kids at the Nook,' said Lord Uffenham, like Doctor Watson saying "Holmes, a child has done this horrid thing!" 'There are three of them, each capable of painting a hundred moustaches on a hundred statues. Twine should watch them closely and be on the alert for clues. Not that he'll get any. Impossible of proof, the whole thing. How's he going to bring it home to anyone? Answer me that.'

It was precisely this that was giving Jane that feeling of bafflement and frustration. She was in the position of the Big Four at Scotland Yard when they know perfectly well that it was Professor Moriarty who put the arsenic in the Ruritanian ambassador's soup but have no means of proving it to the satisfaction of a jury. On such occasions the Big Four knit their brows and bite their lower lips, and Jane knit and bit hers. A momentary urge to bang her uncle on the head with the coffee pot came and passed. It is at such times as these that breeding tells.

But she had other weapons on her armory.

'Did I tell you the kitchen range had gone wrong again?' she asked casually.

'No, has it?'

'You'll have to lunch on sardines.'

Lord Uffenham snorted militantly. The consciousness of having won a moral victory made him strong.

'Like blazes I'll lunch on any bally sardines. Yer know what I'm going to do with you? I'm going to take yer up to London and fill yer to the brim with rich food at Barribault's. We'll go on a regular bender. And after lunch you can saunter down Bond Street, rubbing your nose on the jewellers' windows.'

He could have said nothing more calculated to soothe a fermenting niece. Jane did not often nowadays get a treat like lunch at Barribault's Hotel, that haunt of Texas millionaires and visiting Majarajahs. And if there was one thing she enjoyed, it was window-shopping. Ceasing to be the governess grilling a juvenile suspect, she kissed Lord Uffenham on the top of his bald head.

'That'll be wonderful. I'll have to get back fairly early, though, because I'm having tea with Dora Wimpole. All right, then, we'll leave it that the outrage was the work of an international gang.'

'Yerss, always up to something, those international gangs. Noted for it.'

Well content with this happy ending to an episode which at the outset had threatened to be a bit sticky, Lord Uffenham turned to his *Times*. But having discovered that one of the clues in his crossword puzzle was 'The ointment in short has no point' and another 'No see here, it's a sort of church with a chapter', both beyond the powers of even a Keggs to solve, cast the beastly thing from him and prepared for further conversation.

'What's Twine doing about it?'

'He's rubbing it with turpentine.'

'That'll take it off, will it?'

'He hopes so.'

'Yerss, turpentine ought to do it. That'll be one in the eye for those Nook kids. They won't know which way to look. All their trouble for nothing.'

'I thought we had agreed that it was an international gang that had done it.'

'Or, as you say, one in the eye for the international gang. *They* won't know which way to look. So he was furious about it, was he? I thought I heard him. It sounded like a pig being killed. I will say for Stanhope Twine that whatever his other defects – and they are numerous – they pale into insignificance beside his revolting voice. How yer can stand the feller beats me. Let alone wanting to marry him.'

Usually when the subject of Stanhope Twine came up and the conversation reached this point it was Jane's practice to say her say in no restrained fashion, but today the prospect of lunch at Barribault's had softened her, and it was quite mildly that she suggested that, as they had discussed all that before, there was no need to go into it again.

Lord Uffenham was not to be put off. He considered himself in *loco parentis* to this girl, and her welfare was very near his heart.

'There is every need. I want to save yer from yerself, my good wench. And I want to save myself from having a nephew foisted on me, the mere contemplation of whose bally face gives me a rising sensation of nausea. Lord love a duck, when you get hitched up, I want yer old man to be someone I can drop in on and smoke a pipe with and generally nurse in my bosom. Like young Miller, who married yer sister Anne. I was always in and out of their place, and it has been a lasting grief to me that they pushed off to America and settled there. I miss Walter.'

'You mean Jeff.'

'Is his name Jeff?'

'That's the story he tells.'

'Jeff, yerss, of course. I'm bad at names. I remember, back in the year 1912, getting the push from a girl called Kate because I wrote her a letter beginning "My own darling Mabel". But I was saying . . . What was I saying?'

'That you want me to marry someone you can nurse in your bosom.'

'That's right. Not much to ask of one's niece, I should have thought. But what happens? You come and lay this marble-chipping Gawd-help-us on the mat with a cheery "Hi, everybody, look what I've found". You ought to have more consideration for others, my girl.'

'Nieces can't marry just to give uncles something to nurse in their bosom. They have to think of themselves.'

'Not if they've got the right stuff in them. Did I think of myself? No! I said to myself "This girl isn't yer niece Jane's cup of tea, Uffenham, and you must put Jane's feelings first. Wash her out, my boy, wash her out".'

'Uncle George.'

'Yerss?'

'What on earth are you talking about?'

'I'm talking about my late fiancée.'

'Your *what*?'

'Lord love a duck, you know what a fiancée is. You're one yerself, God help yer. Yerss, I don't mind telling yer, now that the thing's all blown over, that as recently as a couple of weeks ago I was engaged to be married to an usherette called Marlene at the Rivoli cinema at Herne Hill. But I knew she wasn't the sort of girl you would cotton to, so I broke it off.'

Here Lord Uffenham permitted himself a little licence. It was not he but his betrothed who had broken the engagement, she having met a commercial traveller who in looks, dress and general *espièglerie* left his lordship simply nowhere. It had been a great relief to the elderly peer.

Not that he thought of himself as elderly. Except for an occasional twinge of rheumatism when the English summer was more than ordinarily severe, Lord Uffenham still felt like the gay young Guardee he had been in 1912. It was not the fact that he was a little older than he had been forty years ago that had sown doubts in his mind during the period of his betrothal, but the revelation that his affianced was a girl of expensive tastes. It is disquieting for a man who is living on a meagre annuity to discover that he is expected to come through every other day with bottles of scent and boxes of chocolates. A man in such circumstances hears the voice of prudence whispering in his ear and knows that it is talking sense.

'Yerss,' he said, 'I broke it off. She wasn't a girl you'd have cared for, so I sacrificed myself.'

Jane was still gasping.

'*Well!*' she said.

'Quite all right,' said Lord Uffenham, looking like Sidney Carton. 'Got to do the square thing. *Noblesse oblige.*'

'So that's what happens when I let you go for a run by yourself! I shall keep you on a lead in future. Fancy at your age—'

'What d'yer mean, my age?'

'– sneaking off—'

'I resent that word "sneaking".'

'– and getting engaged to usherettes.'

'Not half as bad as getting engaged to sculptors.'

'What on earth made you do such a chuckleheaded thing?'

Actually what had caused Lord Uffenham to plight his troth had been that lifelong habit of his of proposing marriage to girls whenever the conversation seemed to be flagging a bit and a feller felt he had to say *something*. It had got him into trouble before – notably in the years 1912, 1913, 1920 and 1921 – and he saw now that it was a mistake. But he did not mention this to Jane, for he had seen his opportunity to speak the word in season.

'I'll tell yer what made me do it. She was the first pretty girl I'd had a chance of talking to since I came to live down here, so she bowled me over. I was corn before her sickle. And exactly the same thing has happened to you. Yer wouldn't have looked twice at a feller like Twine if yer hadn't been cooped up in a London suburb with nobody else in sight.'

Jane gave a little start. It is always disconcerting when someone else puts into words a thought that has been hovering at the back of one's own mind.

'Nonsense,' she said, but she spoke uncertainly.

Lord Uffenham pressed his attack like a good general. That touch of uncertainty had not escaped him.

'I'll prove it to yer from my own case history. Do you remember your great-aunt Alice? No, she died three years before you were born, so I doubt if you'd ever have met her. She lived in a godforsaken little village on the Welsh border in Shropshire, and my old guv'nor made me go and stay with her one summer. Said there might be money in it. There wasn't, as it turned out, because she left it all to the Society For The Propagation of The Gospel In Foreign Parts, but the point I'm making is that I hadn't been there a week when I got engaged to the sister-in-law of a woman called Postlethwaite, who bred Siamese cats. Purely as the result of ennui and by way of filling in the time somehow. Yours is a parallel case, and I feel it my duty, as an older man than you, to warn yer. Don't dream of marrying that monumental mason just to relieve the monotony of suburban life. If yer do, there'll be a bitter awakening,' said Lord Uffenham, and having delivered this valuable lecture on what a young girl ought to know picked up his *Times* and bent his fine mind to the solving of the clue 'Naked without a penny has the actor become'. And Jane, seeing that he was now beyond the reach of the human voice, went to her room to select a frock which would do the family credit at Barribault's.

Her air was that of a girl who has been given food for thought.

CHAPTER 9

At about the same moment, up in London, Bill Hollister was entering the Gish Galleries.

'Punctual to the dot, you observe, Elphinstone,' he said, 'if you'll excuse a slight touch of smugness. I turned in early last night and got my full eight hours. Hence the sparkling eyes, elastic walk and rosy cheeks, and hence, no doubt, the fact that you look to me once more your own bonny self and not, as was the case yesterday, like a Chinaman with a combination of jaundice and ague. Elphinstone, I've come to the conclusion that we are saps, you and I. We don't know what's good for us. Where do you live?'

'I live with an aunt in Camden Town.'

'If you can call that living. And I hang out off the King's Road, Chelsea. That is why I say that we are saps. We ought both to move to Valley Fields. In that favoured spot you can maintain an establishment on the general lines of that of an Oriental monarch of the better type on next to nothing. I ascertained this last night by personal observation. I was dining there.'

'You do get around, don't you?'

'Yes, I suppose I am something of a social pet. It's probably my affability that does it. I was dining with my club acquaintance Twine, or Spine as you prefer to call him, a man who I should have said was about as impecunious as, if you will pardon the expression, dammit, and I had scarcely crossed the threshold when platoons of butlers sprang out at me from every nook and cranny. You wouldn't be far out in saying that Twine dwells in marble halls with vassals and serfs at his side. And, what is more, he has a cook who is a veritable *cordon bleu*.'

'Eh?'

'I thought that would be above your head, young dumb-bell. I mean that she is a consummate artist. The dinner she dished up last night was of the kind that melts in the mouth and puts hair on the chest. It's a little hard. There is Twine, a mere cipher in the body politic, with a cook like that cooking her head off for him, while I, holding an important executive position in a famous art gallery, and looked up to from one end of Bond Street to the other, dine on leftovers and lunch on bread and cheese.'

'You won't have to have bread and cheese today. Mr Gish said tell you you're to take someone to lunch.'

'Who?'

'I don't know. One of the customers.'

'Clients, girl, clients. Well,' said Bill, not surprised, for Mr Gish, whose digestion had ceased to function satisfactorily in 1947, always preferred to let his assistant entertain the victims for whom he was spreading his net, 'that's fine. I shall enjoy that. I hope the venue will be Barribault's. I haven't been to Barribault's since the day when Pop Gish, coming over all Dickensy as the result of selling a Matisse for six times its proper value, invited me there to celebrate with him. Would this, do you suppose, be a client important enough to justify a Barribault's orgy?'

'You'd better ask him. He wants to see you.'

'Who wouldn't? Well, I think I can give him five minutes. But you realize what this means, Elphinstone? It means that you will have to do without me for awhile. Come, come, woman, stop crying like that. When the fields are white with daisies, I'll return.'

In the main gallery Mr Gish, small, dark and irascible, in appearance and temperament rather like a salamander, was standing before the statuette of a nude lady who appeared to be practising some sort of dance step. He was flicking at it with a feather duster, and Bill raised his hat, always the chivalrous gentleman.

'Is this man annoying you, madam?' he asked, courteously.

The sound of that familiar voice seemed to affect the proprietor of the Gish Galleries like an unexpected alligator bite in the lower limbs. He spun on his axis, eyes blazing through their horn-rimmed spectacles, and, like Miss Elphinstone on a similar occasion, said 'Ho!'

'So you've condescended to come here, have you?'

'And right on time, chief, as you may have noticed.'

'Where the devil were you yesterday?'

Bill raised a hand.

'Never mind yesterday. As the poet says, "Every day is a fresh beginning, Every morn is the world made anew. Yesterday's errors let yesterday cover." Today is another day, and here I am, alert, keen-eyed and on my toes, all eagerness to learn what's cooking.'

As so often happened when he found himself in conference with his young assistant, two conflicting emotions were warring within Mr Gish – one an imperious urge to fire him on the spot, the other an uneasy feeling that to do so would be to label himself an ingrate. Twenty-six years ago, in the spacious days of 1929, Bill's father, who had more money then than he knew what to do with, had given Mr Gish some of it to start this business of his, and a conscientious man cannot lightly ignore such an obligation. Bill, too, was a good assistant, if you could stand his affability, a definite improvement on some of the wooden-headed morons whom Mr Gish had employed in his time. If you told him to do something, he did not gape at you like a weak-minded fish, he went and did it – and did it, moreover, without messing everything up. He had a good picture-side manner, and clients liked him. There was something about his honest, open face and the cauliflower ear which had accrued to him as the result of his amateur boxing that inspired trust.

Weighing these things, Mr Gish decided not to cleanse his bosom of the perilous stuff that was weighing on his heart, and Bill proceeded.

'I hear you want me to give one of the local lepers lunch. Who is it this time?'

'He's a big paint-and-enamel man. His name's McColl. I've sold him my Boudin, and I'm hoping he'll buy my Degas.'

'He will if the suavity of my small talk and a hell of a good lunch can swing it. I think nothing meaner than Barribault's for a big paint-and-enamel man, don't you?'

'Yes, take him to Barribault's. Tell Miss Elphinstone to book a table.'

'I will. And while on the subject of Elphinstone, she was say-ing something about your wanting me to go and look at some pictures.'

'Oh, those pictures, yes. Were they any good?'

'I have yet to see them.' Mr Gish started.

'What do you mean? Didn't you go?'

'I couldn't. I was feeling much too frail. I think I may have been overworking lately. Tell me about them.'

For an instant it seemed that the man at the helm of the Gish Galleries was about to forget his obligations to Mr Hollister senior, but his better self rose to the surface and with a strong effort he succeeded in suppressing the words that rose to his lips.

'They belong to Lord Uffenham. There was a girl in here the day before yesterday—'

'They can't keep away from you, can they, poor fluttering moths.'

'A Miss Benedick. Lord Uffenham's niece. She says he wants me to sell these pictures for him. They are down at his place in the country, Shipley Hall, near Tonbridge.'

'No, there, with the deepest respect, me lud, you're wrong. Shipley Hall is the rural seat of my old buddy, Roscoe Bunyan. I heard him telling someone so at our mutual club the other day. You don't know Roscoe, do you? He looks like a cartoon of Capital in the *Daily Worker*. Country butter, no doubt. He probably eats it by the pound at Shipley Hall, which, as I said before, belongs to him and not to this Lord Uffenham of whom you speak.'

'Lord Uffenham has let Shipley Hall to him.'

'Oh, I see. That throws a different light on the matter.'

'After you've given McColl lunch, go there and look at those pictures.'

'Why don't you?'

'I have to go to Brighton.'

'Always off on a jaunt somewhere, aren't you? It's always the way. Everybody works but Father.'

Mr Gish counted ten slowly. Once again his better self had attempted to get away from him.

'To a sale,' he said coldly.

'Oh, to a sale?'

'Yes, to a sale.'

'Well, it makes a good story,' said Bill a little dubiously. 'All right, while you are out with the boys, burning up Brighton, I will kiss McColl good-bye and drive to this Shipley Hall of which I have heard so much. Where do I find you, to communicate with you?'

'I shall be at the Hotel Metropole from four o'clock on.'

'I see. In the bar, of course.'

'In the *lounge*. I am having tea with a client.'

'Female, one presumes. What, I ask myself, is the secret of this mysterious attraction? Very well, I will give you a buzz as soon as I have formed an opinion of these pictures. And may I say how gratified I am that you should be entrusting me with this important commission. Bless my soul, you must have great confidence in me.'

'I haven't any confidence in you. And I don't want you to form an opinion, as you call it. All you have to do is to ask Mortimer Bayliss what he thinks of them.'

'Mortimer Bayliss? Is he at Shipley Hall? I ran into him last night.'

'Well, you'll run into him again this afternoon. Ask him what he feels about them. There isn't a better judge of pictures in the world.'

'And what a beautiful world it is, is it not? Let me tell you how it strikes me. I look about me, and I say to myself—'

But Mr Gish, never able to stay in one place for long, particularly if it involved conversing with his affable assistant, had vanished.

The morning's work proceeded much as on other mornings. Mrs Weston-Smythe came in, saw – in the order named – the 'Follower of El Greco', the 'Diaz Flower-Piece' and the 'Pupil of The Master Of The Holy Kinship Of Cologne', and then, when her spirits were at their lowest ebb, was shown the 'Bernardo Daddi', which she bought. At one o'clock Bill took hat in hand, gave his cutaway coat a flick with the whisk broom, and prepared to make his way to Barribault's, greatly stimulated by the thought of the slap-up lunch that admirable eating-house was going to give him at the firm's expense.

In the outer office Miss Elphinstone was at the telephone.

'Oh, just a minute,' she said, as she saw Bill. She put a hand over the mouthpiece. 'It's a girl.'

'And I had always wanted a boy. Too bad.'

'Do you know anything about some pictures?'

'I know everything about all pictures.'

'It's a Miss Benedick about some pictures she says she saw Mr Gish about them the day before yesterday belonging to her uncle, Lord Buffenham.'

'Ye gods, child, your syntax! What you mean, I presume, is that a Miss Benedick is calling with reference to certain paintings at present the property of her uncle, Lord Uffenham – not Buffenham – concerning which she has been in conference with my employer with a view to his selling them. Yes, I've been briefed about those. Out of the way, Elphinstone, let me grapple with this. Hello? Miss Benedick?'

'Oh, good morning. I'm speaking for my uncle, Lord Uffenham,' said a voice, and Bill nearly dropped the receiver.

For the voice was a voice in a million, a voice that cast a spell and wooed the ear to listen, a voice that stole into a man's heart and stirred him up as with a ten-foot pole. He had never in his life heard anything that made so instant an appeal to him, and strange thrills ran up his spine and out at the roots of his hair.

With difficulty he contrived to speak.

'Was . . . was it about those pictures of Lord Uffenham's?'

'Yes.'

'Down at Shipley Hall?'

'Yes.'

'You called here about them the other day.'

'Yes.'

Bill wished that she would not confine herself to mono-syllables. He wanted long, lovely sentences.

'I'm going to Shipley Hall this afternoon to look at them.'

'Oh, good. Who are you?'

'Mr Gish's assistant. Ah, shut up, woman.'

'I beg your pardon?'

'I'm sorry. I was addressing the fatheaded lady receptionist at my elbow. She said she betted I couldn't say "Mr Gish's assistant" ten times quick.'

'And can you?'

'I'm not sure.'

'Well, do try. And thank you ever so much. I'll tell my uncle.'

Bill replaced the receiver dazedly. He was feeling as if he had passed through some great emotional experience, as indeed he had. It amazed him that Miss Elphinstone, who also had had the privilege of hearing that lovely voice, should be sitting there calm and unmoved, and not only calm and unmoved but chewing gum.

Bill Hollister was unusually sensitive to beauty in the human voice. One of the reasons why he preferred not to see too much of Stanhope Twine was that the latter, when he felt strongly on any subject, was inclined to squeal and gibber like the sheeted dead in the Roman streets a little ere the mightiest Julius fell. And he could, he sometimes thought, have borne with more equanimity Miss Murphrey's comparison of him to a sheep dog operating a funeral parlour as a side line, had her vocal delivery less closely resembled that of a peahen.

The voice to which he had been listening and which was still echoing down the corridors of his soul had been a magic voice, a round, soft, liquid voice, a voice to appease a traffic policeman or soothe an inland revenue official. He felt as if he had been in telephonic communication with an angel, one probably the mainstay of the celestial choir, and there rose before his mental eye a picture. The scene was a church, and he, in a cutaway coat and striped trousers, was walking down the aisle with this silver-voiced girl on his arm while the organ played 'Oh, Perfect Love' and the spectators in the ringside pews whispered 'What a charming couple!' A Bishop and assistant clergy had done their stuff, the returns were all in, and she was his ... his ... his ... for better and for worse, in sickness and in health, till death did them ...

At this point it occurred to him that he had not the pleasure of her acquaintance, or any reasonable hope of making it. There was, he reflected, always something. Moodily he passed out into Bond Street and, directing his steps eastward, was presently seated with Mr McColl at a table in Barribault's glittering dining-room.

The lunch was not one of those festive lunches, though Barribault's, as always, spared no effort to make it go. Bill had no means of knowing what was the norm or average of sprightliness among big paint-and-enamel men, but an hour spent in his society inclined him to think that Mr McColl was below rather than above it. He was a strong silent paint-and-enamel man, who tucked into his food with a fine appetite, but contributed little or nothing to the feast of reason and the flow of soul beyond an occasional grunt, seeming to be brooding on the last lot of enamel or yesterday's consignment of paint. Bill in consequence had had to work a good deal harder than he could have wished, especially at a moment when his spirits were low and his mind preoccupied. It was a relief to him when his guest rose to go and he was able to escort him to the swing doors and leave him there in the care of the Ruritanian Field-Marshal who gets taxis for Barribault's clientele.

As he turned back into the lobby, his spirits were still low, nor, despite the fact that he had seen the last of Mr McColl, is this to be wondered at. It is generally supposed that the depths of human frustration are plumbed by the man who is all dressed up and no place to go, and few, contemplating such a man, are so callous as not to heave a sigh and drop the tear of pity. But though that dressy unfortunate is unquestionably in a nasty spot and entitled to beat his breast like the wedding guest when he heard the loud bassoon, his sufferings are a good deal less acute than those of one who, all eagerness to pour out the treasures of a rich nature on the girl he loves, is debarred from doing so by the circumstance that he does not know where she lives or what she looks like.

A consuming desire to smoke came upon Bill. He reached for his cigarette case and found it was not there. He must, he supposed, have left it on the table, and he hurried back to the restaurant to retrieve it before some Maharajah who liked nice things saw and pocketed it.

To get to the table which he had been occupying he had to pass one where there was sitting a small, fair-haired girl, at whom he cast a fleeting glance. And he was moving on, having classified her mentally as 'rather pretty', when she spoke, addressing a passing bus boy.

'Will you ask the head waiter to come here, please,' she said, and Bill, having started convulsively as if the management of Barribault's had thrust a skewer into the fleshy part of his leg, not that they would, became as rigid as ever Lord Uffenham had become when falling into one of his trances. He had the momentary illusion that the management of Barribault's, however foreign to their normal policy such an action would have been, had hit him over the head with a sock full of wet sand.

CHAPTER 10

In the actual line 'Will you ask the head-waiter to come here, please' there is nothing, one would say, calculated to stun the senses and cause the hearer to stiffen in every limb. It is the sort of throw-away line a dramatist would give to one of his minor characters at the beginning of the Act Three supper scene to cover the noise of the customers stumbling back into the auditorium after the intermission and tripping over other people's feet. It misses the Aristotelian ideal of pity and terror by a wide margin.

What had congealed Bill where he stood had not been the words themselves but the voice that had spoken them. He refused to believe that in a smallish city like London there could co-exist two such magic voices. With eyes protruding to their fullest extent he stared at this fair-haired, rather pretty girl, and noted that her charms had become enhanced by a flush which, in his opinion, was most attractive. Many girls, even in these sophisticated days, find themselves flushing when human snails halt beside the table where they are lunching and stand goggling at them with their eyes sticking six inches out of the parent sockets. Giving this snail-impersonator a look such as a particularly fastidious princess might have given the caterpillar which she had discovered in her salad, Jane averted her gaze, and was continuing to avert it, when the uncouth intruder spoke.

'Miss Benedick?' he said, in a low, hoarse voice which would have interested a throat specialist, and Jane turned like a startled kitten, her flush now the blush of shame and embarrassment. For the first time in the last quarter of an hour she was thankful that her Uncle George was not with her, for he was a stern critic of this sort of thing. 'Hell's bells,' her Uncle George had often said to her, waggling his eyebrows to lend emphasis to his words, 'yer've *got* to remember people, my girl, or yer'll be about as popular as a ruddy ant at a picnic. Nothing makes fellers rattier than having wenches not know them from Adam next time they meet.'

And now that she looked at this young man, seeing him steadily and seeing him whole, there did come to her a faint glimmering of a recollection of having met him before some-where ... at some long-ago Hunt Ball, perhaps, or some distant garden party, or possibly in some previous existence. That hair of his, ginger in colour and looking as if he had brushed it a week ago last Wednesday, seemed somehow to strike a chord, as did his eyes, which, she now saw, were very pleasant eyes. She was goading her memory to dredge from its depths a name, and memory, as always on these occasions, was shrugging its shoulders and giving the thing up as a bad job, when he spoke again.

'We were talking on the telephone this morning. About Lord Uffenham's pictures. I'm at the Gish Galleries.'

A wave of relief swept over Jane. No girl can be expected to remember people, if they have simply been anonymous voices on the telephone. She had not failed that male Emily Post, her Uncle George, after all, and this healing thought lent such animation to her manner that Bill's interior organs were for the second time stirred up by that invisible ten-foot pole. He was wondering how he could ever have labelled this girl in his mind as 'rather pretty'. It was as though some traveller, seeing the Taj Mahal by moonlight for the first time, had described it in a letter home as a fairly decent-looking sort of tomb.

'Of course! You're Mr Gish's assistant. Do sit down,' said Jane.

Bill sat down, glad to do so, for he was feeling a little dizzy. Her last words had been accompanied by a smile, and the effect of it had been devastating. His only coherent thought, as he took his seat, was that a lifetime devoted to waiting and watching for that smile would be a lifetime well spent.

Jane was puzzled.

'But how,' she asked, 'did you know who I was?'

'I recognized your voice.'

'Recognized my voice?' Jane stared. 'After half a dozen words on the telephone?'

'One would have been ample,' said Bill. He had now got over his initial nervousness and was feeling his affable self once more. 'It is a lovely, unique voice, in a class of its own and once heard never forgotten, limpid as a woodland brook and vibrant with all the music of the spheres. When you asked that child in the apron with the gravy spots on it to send the head-waiter along, one could fancy one was listening to silver bells tinkling across the foam of perilous seas in faery lands forlorn.'

'Seas *where*?'

'In faery lands forlorn. Not my own. Keats.'

'Oh? Well, that's good, isn't it?'

'Couldn't be better,' agreed Bill cordially.

Jane had become conscious of a certain uneasiness. Usually an adept at keeping ardent youth at a safe distance, she had begun to wonder if her technique would be sound enough to serve her here. Many young men in their time had said nice things to her, but none with the ecstatic fervour which had animated the remarks of this one. He gave the impression of speaking straight from the heart, and a large, throbbing heart at that. A well-read young man, too. Keats and everything. She remembered another of her Uncle George's *obiter dicta*. 'When they start talking poetry at yer,' that deep thinker had once warned her, 'watch yer step like billy-o, my girl.'

And what was making her uneasy was that she was not at all sure that she wanted to watch her step. She was feeling strangely drawn to this man who had come crashing into her life and who had now for some moments been gazing at her with the uninhibited enthusiasm of a small boy confronted with a saucer of ice-cream. She liked his hair, though not blind to the fact that it could have done with a couple of licks from a pair of military brushes. She liked his eyes, which were as friendly and honest as any eyes she had ever looked into. She liked everything about him . . . and far more warmly, her conscience told her, than a girl who was engaged to Stanhope Twine ought to be doing. A girl engaged to Stanhope Twine should, it pointed out, experience this odd sensation of breathlessness only when it was Stanhope Twine who had induced it. That a ginger-headed young man, whom she had never seen till five minutes ago, should be causing her to feel as if she were floating on a pink cloud and listening to the music of a particularly good orchestra was, her conscience suggested in that unpleasant way which consciences have, all wrong.

With a feeling that there was much in what it said and that the emotional content of the conversation should without delay be reduced, she turned it to a safer subject.

'So you're really going to Shipley this afternoon to see those pictures of Uncle George's?' she said. 'I must say I envy you. It's a lovely place, especially at this time of year. I miss it terribly.'

'You've not been there lately?'

'Not for ages.'

'You were there as a child?'

'All the time.'

Bill's eyes closed in a sort of ecstasy.

'How wonderful it will be, seeing all the little spots and nooks where you wandered as a child,' he said devoutly. 'I shall feel I am on holy ground.'

Jane perceived that in supposing that she had found a safer subject she had erred. She tried another.

'That head-waiter seems a long time coming,' she said.

Bill, who had intended to speak further and at some length, blinked as if he had been sauntering down the street and had walked into a lamp-post. It pained him that she should wish to talk of head-waiters, for it lowered the conversation to a prosaic plane which he deprecated, but, if such was her desire, he must indulge it.

'Oh, yes, you want to see him, don't you?'

'Actually I don't in the least, but I'm afraid I've got to.'

'What's the trouble?'

'I can't pay the bill.'

'Lost your purse?'

'No, I've got my purse, but there's nothing in it. Would you care to hear my story?'

'I'm all agog.'

'My uncle invited me to lunch . . .'

'According to Nancy Mitford, you should say "luncheon", but go on.'

'The arrangement was that he would look in at his club and meet me here at one, and we would then luncheon together at his expense. When he hadn't turned up by half past, I couldn't hold out any longer. So I came in and luncheoned by myself.'

'Paying no attention to the prices in the right-hand colunm?'

'Ignoring them completely. I thought it would be all right and that he was bound to arrive, but he hasn't. I know just what has happened. He has got talking with the boys, as he calls them, and forgotten all about me.'

'Absent-minded?'

'Not exactly absent-minded, but he gets absorbed in things. He's probably deep in a discussion of the apostolic claims of the church of Abyssinia or something. Or else he's telling them why greyhounds are called greyhounds. He found that out in the evening paper yesterday, and it thrilled him.'

'Why are they?'

'Because grey is the old English word for badger, and grey-hounds were used in hunting the badger.'

'I thought they hunted electric hares.'

'Only when they can't get badgers. And anyway, however they pass their time, it doesn't alter the fact that here I am, penniless. Well, not quite penniless, but certainly two-pounds-fiveless.'

'You think that is what the bruise will amount to?'

'About that. I rather let myself go.'

'Quite rightly. It's a poor heart that never rejoices, and one's only young once, I often say. Then all is well. I can manage two pounds five.'

'You? But you can't pay for my lunch.'

'Of course I can pay for your luncheon. Who's to stop me?'

'Not I, for one. You've saved my life.'

'Just the Gish Galleries service.'

The magnificent form of the head-waiter materialized at their side. Bill gave him a lordly look.

'*L'addition,*' he said haughtily.

'Yes, sir,' said the head-waiter. Jane drew a reverent breath.

'Just like that!' she said. 'And in French!'

'One drops into it, I find. Unconsciously, as it were.'

'Do you speak it fluently?'

'Very, what I know of it. Which is just that word "*l'addition*", and, of course, "*Oo là là!*".'

'I can't remember even as much as that. And I had a French governess. Where did you study?'

'In Paris, when I was learning to paint.'

'Oh, so *that's* why you don't brush your hair.'

'I beg your pardon?'

'I mean because you're an artist.'

'I'm not an artist. Not now. My soul belongs to Pop Gish of the Gish Galleries.'

'What a shame!'

'Oh, it's not a bad life. I like Gish. What Gish thinks of me, I couldn't tell you. From time to time I seem to sense something in his manner that suggests that he may be feeling the strain a little.'

'How did you come to get into a job like that?'

'It's a long story, but I think I can condense it into a short-short. I was in London a good deal during the war as a G.I. and got very fond of it, and after I had gone home and worked at various things and saved a bit of money I came back on a sort of sentimental pilgrimage. When my money ran out, which was considerably sooner than I had foreseen, I had to find a job, and your choice of jobs when you are in a foreign country without a labour permit is rather limited. You don't get the cream of what's going.'

'I suppose not.'

'So when I ran into Gish, who was an old friend of my father's, and he offered me sanctuary in his thieves' kitchen, I jumped at it.'

'How did you run into him?'

'In the process of hawking my pictures around every gallery in town. His was about the forty-seventh I visited. He took me on, and I've been working there ever since.'

'But you'd rather be painting?'

'If I had lots of money, I'd do nothing else. What would you do if you had lots of money?'

Jane reflected.

'Well, I'd start by fixing up Uncle George at Shipley again. He does hate it so, not being able to live there. After that . . . I think I'd come and luncheon at Barribault's every day.'

'Me, too. It's a great place.'

'Yes.'

'Wonderful cooking.'

'Marvellous. And one meets such interesting people. Ah!'

'Yes?'

'A waiter is sneaking up behind you with a little tray in his hand. No doubt containing the bad news.'

'Or the kiss of death, as I sometimes call it.'

'Are you sure you can pay it?'

'Just this once. You mustn't rely on me as a general thing. There,' said Bill, as the waiter withdrew. '*Oo là là!* The shadow has passed.'

'And a great weight has rolled from my mind. I don't know how to thank you. My preserver! What do you think would have happened if you hadn't come riding up on your white horse? What would they have done to me?'

'It's difficult to say. I don't know how they handle these things in a place like Barribault's. My only experience of a similar nature has been in a rather more rugged establishment, many years ago when I was a slip of a boy. I boyishly slipped the bad news to the management after a hearty meal of hot dogs and ice-cream that I was unable to meet my financial obligations, and a fellow in shirt sleeves of about the build of Rocky Marciano grabbed me by the scruff of the neck and kicked me fourteen times. I was then set to washing dishes.'

'How awful!'

'But educative. Tried in the furnace, I came out of that kitchen a graver, deeper boy.'

'Where was this?'

'At a joint called Archie's Diner, Good Eats, over in America, not far from a place of the name of Meadowhampton.'

'What! Did you say Meadowhampton?'

'Yes. It's on Long Island.'

'But how extraordinary!'

'Why?'

'It's my home town.'

Bill looked at her incredulously.

'You mean you *know* Meadowhampton? This is astounding. I wouldn't have thought anyone outside America had ever heard of it. When were you there?'

'Ages ago. When I was a slip of a girl. I was sent over to America at the beginning of the war.'

'Oh, I see.'

'I remember every bit of it. Straw's paper shop, the Patio Inn, the drugstore, the movie house, the library, the Swordfish Club . . . I loved Meadowhampton. It seems so odd that it should have pursued me to England.'

'Would you call it pursuing?'

'Oh, I don't mean you. Someone from there has taken Shipley.'

'Roscoe Bunyan.'

'That's right. So you know him? What a pity. I wanted to say all sorts of unpleasant things about him. But if he's a friend of yours—'

'I wouldn't say exactly a friend. We belong to the same club and exchange a word or two occasionally, but we are not social equals. He's rich, I'm just one of the dregs. He isn't such a bad fellow, though. I rather like him.'

'Then you must like everybody.'

Bill thought this over. It was a novel idea, but there was truth in it.

'I suppose I do.'

'I see. Just another George.'

'Another who?'

'Our bulldog.'

'Is he a glad-hander?'

'Very much so. If we ever have a burglar, George will put him at his ease in a moment. The perfect host. But, you can't really like Roscoe Bunyan?'

'I don't dislike him. I did as a boy, I remember.'

'I'm not surprised. He was a loathsome boy.'

'He was, wasn't he? Very much the Bunyan heir. I nearly beat him up once.'

'How wonderful. Why was that? Did he steal your all-day sucker?'

'We differed on a point of policy. There was a wretched little rat of a girl spending the summer at Meadowhampton, and Roscoe thought the done thing was to hold her under water in the swimming pool till her eyes popped. I took a conflicting view and told him – speaking sternly – that if he ever did it again. . . .'

Barribault's restaurant is solidly built, but to Jane it seemed that it had suddenly began to float about her. The head-waiter, passing at the moment, had the aspect of a head-waiter dancing the shimmy.

'It can't be!' she cried. 'I don't believe it! It isn't really *you*?'

Bill could make nothing of this. She was leaning forward, her eyes shining.

'Don't tell me you're Bill Hollister!'

'Yes, but—?'

'I'm the rat,' said Jane.

CHAPTER 11

Bill blinked.

'The rat?'

'The wretched little rat.'

'You?'

'Yes.'

'You mean ... *you* are?'

'That's right. The one who was for ever blowing bubbles ... when Roscoe Bunyan held her under water.'

Bill stared across the table. He looked at her fixedly for a moment, and shook his head.

'No,' he said. 'It doesn't make sense. The rat to whom you allude ... What was her name?'

'Jane.'

'That's right. As I recall her, she had a face that would have stopped a clock.'

'I stopped dozens, in my prime. I didn't know my own strength.'

'Her mouth looked like the back of a telephone switchboard.'

'I had to wear braces on my teeth, to straighten them.'

'She was heavily spectacled.'

'Until my twelfth year, glasses were prescribed to correct a slight strabismus.'

'And why do I remember nothing of that divine voice?'

'I don't suppose it was divine then. Probably squeaky.'

Bill continued dazed.

'This,' he said, 'has come as a great surprise.'

'I thought it might.'

'Do you mind if I have a small beaker of brandy?'

'Go ahead.'

'And for you?'

'Nothing, thanks.'

Bill caught the waiter's eye, and gave his order. 'I'm rather shaken,' he explained. 'I still have a feeling you're pulling my leg.'

'No, that's my story, and I stick to it.'

'You really are . . . ?'

'Yes, really.'

Bill drew a deep breath.

'But, good heavens, it's incredible. The mind boggles. I mean, look at you now. You're . . .'

'Yes?'

'You're beautiful . . . lovely . . . wonderful . . . marvellous . . . a radiant vision. The child Jane could have made good money scaring crows in the cornfields of Minnesota, and you, . . . why, you begin where Helen of Troy left off.'

'All done with mirrors.'

The waiter brought the brandy, and Bill drained it at a gulp

'You should sip it,' said Jane maternally.

'Sip it? When my whole nervous system is doing buck-and-wing dances? A weaker man would have called for the cask.'

'I'm afraid I've upset you.'

'I wouldn't call it upsetting so much. It's more like . . . no, I don't know how to describe it.'

'Has everything gone black?'

'Just the opposite. It is as if sunshine were pouring through the roof and all the waiters and bus boys singing close harmony at the top of their voices. I can't get over it that you should have remembered me all these years.'

'How could I forget you? You were my dream boy. I adored you with a passion I cannot hope to express.'

'You *did*?'

'I worshipped you. I used to follow you about, just gazing at you and wondering how anything so perfect could possibly exist. When you dived off the high-board, I would look up at you from the shallow end and whisper "My hero!" I would have died for one little rose from your hair.'

Bill drew another deep breath.

'You might have mentioned it.'

'I was far too modest. I deemed it best not to tell my love, but to let concealment like a worm i' the bud feed on my damask cheek. Not my own. Shakespeare. Besides, what would have been the use? You wouldn't have looked at me. Or, if you had, it would have been with a shudder.'

Bill was still having trouble with his breathing. He had become conscious of a marked respiratory embarrassment with an absence of endotracheal oxygenation. His voice, when he was able to speak, was husky. That throat specialist, had he been present, would have given him a sharp look, scenting custom.

'So that was how you felt about me! And here we are, meeting again like this. I'd call it fate, wouldn't you?'

'Curious, anyway.'

'No, it's fate, and it's never any use trying to buck fate. You aren't married, are you? No, of course you aren't. It was Miss Benedick, wasn't it? Fine! Capital! Splendid!'

'Why so pleased?'

'Because . . . Because . . . This is possibly going to seem a little sudden, so keep steadily before you the fact that the whole thing was destined from the beginning of time, and it is not for us to throw a spanner into the designs of destiny. Jane,' said Bill, leaning forward and placing a hand on hers. 'Jane . . .'

'Hello, hello, so there yer are,' said a voice. There had loomed up beside the table something large and pear-shaped with heavy eyebrows and a guilty look. 'Bit late, ain't I?' it said, speaking bluffly but avoiding its niece's eye. 'I got talking to a chap at the club.'

If this had been a picnic and Lord Uffenham the ant of which he had spoken in that powerful passage quoted on an earlier page, his intrusion could scarcely have been less welcome to the young man whose well-phrased speech he had interrupted. Bill turned, scowling darkly, and having turned sat gaping. Distinctive and individual were the adjectives that sprang to the lips of anyone wishing to describe Lord Uffenham's appearance, and he had no difficulty in recognizing him as his crony of last night. And the thought that if he had only fraternized with the man more heartily, leaving him no option but to ask him to come in and have a drink, he would have met Jane several hours earlier was so poignant as to deprive him of speech. Each Janeless hour was, in the opinion of William Hollister, an hour wasted and gone down the drain.

Jane, though the head of the family would have preferred it otherwise, had not been deprived of speech.

'Uncle George . . .' she said.

'About this new rabbit disease, this myx-whatever-its-dashed-name-is,' proceeded Lord Uffenham, still avoiding the eye.

'Absorbing subject. Did yer know that foxes, there being now a nation-wide shortage of rabbits, have taken to eating frogs? This club chap assures me it's a fact. They pursue them in packs all over the countryside.'

Jane was not to be diverted into a discussion of the dietary arrangements of foxes. Foxes, as far as she was concerned, could eat cake.

'Uncle George,' she said, and her voice was cold, 'are you aware, you frightful old uncle, that if it had not been for Bill Hollister here, the management of Barribault's would have grabbed me by the scruff of the neck, kicked me fourteen times and set me to work washing dishes?'

'Lord love a duck! What would they do that for?'

'It's an old Barribault custom when girls eat large meals and can't pay for them. Fortunately Bill descended from a cloud in the nick of time, and saved me from the fate that is worse than death. You owe him two pounds ten. Fork out.'

Lord Uffenham forked out.

'Thank yer, my boy,' he said graciously. 'Very civil of yer...'

His voice trailed away. He, too, had recognized his crony of last night, and the thought of how much depended on this crony's secrecy and silence sent his heart sinking into those substantial boots of his. He was up against that old business of 'Where were you on the night of June the twenty-second?' that had so often undone members of the criminal classes to which he belonged. One word from this young man to the effect that they had met and conversed in the garden of Peacehaven on the night of the bearding of Stanhope Twine's statue, and his name would not be Uffenham, but mud. He caught Bill's eye and threw his whole soul into a glance of agonized appeal.

Bill, though mystified, did not fail him.

'Not at all,' he said. 'Only too glad I was able to help. It's very interesting meeting you, Lord Uffenham—'

'For the first time,' interjected that underworld character hastily.

'For the first time,' said Bill, 'because I'm the man the Gish Galleries are sending down to look at your pictures.'

'Really? Well, I'm dashed.'

'He's Mr Gish's assistant ... Mr Gish's assistant ... Mr Sish's ... I knew it couldn't be done,' said Jane. 'Tell him about the pictures.'

'Yes, I'd like to hear about the pictures,' said Bill.

Lord Uffenham mused for a moment. His heart was back in its right place again and bursting with devotion and gratitude to this splendid young feller whose ready intelligence had saved him from the soup into which it had seemed that he must inevitably be plunged. He had never met a young feller he liked more. He had not supposed they made young fellers like that nowadays.

'Well, they're ...' He paused, seeking the *mot juste*. 'They're pictures, if yer know what I mean. When yer going to look at them?'

'Right away. I'm driving down.'

'I'll come with yer.'

'Splendid. You too?'

'No, sorry,' said Jane. 'I promised an old school friend I would have tea with her, and I can't put her off.'

'Why not?'

'She's a very old school friend. Almost decrepit.'

'And we don't want any bally girls around,' said Lord Uffenham gallantly. 'Give me a couple of minutes for a spot of lunch, my boy, and I'll be with yer.'

'I'll go and get the car.'

'Do. Yer'll find me waiting out in the street. Yer can't miss me. Yerss,' said Lord Uffenham, 'it's a fact. Foxes, no longer able to get the daily rabbit, now eat frogs. Like,' he added, driving home his point, 'a lot of ruddy Frenchmen.'

As foreshadowed, Lord Uffenham was waiting in the street when Bill returned with the car. He was deep in conversation with the Ruritanian Field-Marshal at the door. The chap at the club, so informative about rabbits, had also spoken at some length on the sister subject of eels, and Lord Uffenham, who believed in handing these things on, was bringing the Field-Marshal abreast of the eel situation in the south of England, one fraught with interest.

'Yerss,' he was saying, 'according to this feller – Pargiter his name is, though I don't suppose yer know him – the streams down there are so full of the little blighters that the water has taken on the consistency of jelly.'

'Coo,' said the Field-Marshal.

'Three inches long they are, and they have white stomachs.'

'Cor,' said the Field-Marshal.

'Never been in the West Indies, have yer?'

The Field-Marshal said he had not.

'Well, that's where they're born, and when they're old enough, they come to England. Though why the hell they should want to come to England, with a Labour Government likely to get in at any moment, is more than I can tell yer.'

These unfortunately proved to be fighting words. The harmony which had been prevailing, until now perfect, was rudely jarred. The Field-Marshal, stiffening and drawing himself up to his full height of approximately six feet eleven inches, informed Lord Uffenham that he invariably voted the Labour ticket – wishing, he explained, to save the land he loved from the domination of a lot of blinking Fascists, and Lord Uffenham said the Field-Marshal ought to lose no time in having his head examined, because anybody with an ounce more sense than a child with water on the brain knew that those Labour blisters were nothing but a bunch of bally Bolsheviks. And the political argument that ensued – with Lord Uffenham accusing the Field-Marshal of being in the pay of Moscow and the Field-Marshal reminding Lord Uffenham that Mr Aneurin Bevan had described him and the likes of him as lower than vermin – was beginning to verge on the heated, when it was interrupted by the tooting of Bill's klaxon.

It was a ruffled Lord Uffenham who climbed into the car and took his seat, causing Bill, at the wheel, to shoot some inches into the air. It was the sixth Viscount's practice, when intending to sit, to hover poised for a moment and then, relaxing limply, to come down with a bump, like an avalanche.

The opening stages of the drive were conducted in silence, for Bill was thinking of Jane and Lord Uffenham of all the good things he could have said to the Field-Marshal, if only he had thought of them. But after a mile or so the agony of dwelling on what might have been abated, and it occurred to him that he had not yet expressed his gratitude to his young friend for having so intelligently refrained from spilling the beans at the recent get-together. He proceeded to repair the omission.

'Great presence of mind yer showed back there at Barribault's, my boy,' he said. 'When yer stated yer'd never seen me before,' he explained. 'Touch and go it was for a moment.'

Bill was glad this mystery was going to be cleared up. It had been bothering him.

'Oh, yes. I was rather wondering about that. I read the message in your eye, but I couldn't understand it. Why were you so anxious to avoid any touch of auld lang syne?'

'I'll tell yer. Throw yer mind back. Remember that statue of Twine's, the one of the stout female with no clothes on?'

'Vividly.'

'We agreed it was an eyesore?'

'We did.'

'Well, when we ran into each other last night, I'd just been painting a beard on it.'

'A beard?'

'A small imperial beard. With black paint.'

'Oh, I see. Yes, very sensible. Most judicious.'

'You approve?'

'Wholeheartedly.'

'I thought yer would. You're broadminded. But my niece Jane isn't, and if she'd found out I'd been in that garden, she'd have put two and two together and there'd have been hell to pay. Jane's a good girl—'

'She's an angel.'

Lord Uffenham considered this.

'Yerss, I suppose yer could call her that, stretching the facts a little, but she's like all women, it's fatal to let her get the goods on yer. Women never forget. They're worse than elephants. If that statue job had been brought home to me, I'd never have heard the last of it. She'd have touched on it at intervals for the rest of her life. Her mother was that way. My sister Beatrice. I've known my sister Beatrice to bring up things that happened fifty years ago, when we were tots together in our mutual nursery.

"I wouldn't have a second helping of that fruit salad, if I were you, George",' said Lord Uffenham, assuming for purposes of voice-similitude a high falsetto. ' "Yer know how weak yer stomach is. Remember how sick yer were at the Montgomerys' Christmas party in 1901." Thet sort of thing. It's the kind of crisis one wants, if possible, to avoid. So I'm extremely grateful to yer, my boy.'

'Only too glad to have done my bit. We men must stick together.'

'Yerss. Solid front. It's the only way,' said Lord Uffenham, and went into a trance. The impression he conveyed was that he had unhitched his mind and was giving it a complete rest, but that this was not the case was shown by his first words as – some miles later – he came to life again. Turning on his broad base and fixing his pale blue eyes on Bill, he said:

'Angel, did yer say?'

'I beg your pardon?'

'Jane. I think I heard yer say she was an angel?'

'Oh, Jane? Yes, definitely an angel. No argument about that.'

'Known her long?'

'We were tots together in America.'

'Back in 1939?'

'Yes.'

'Seen much of her since?'

'Nothing, until today.'

'Yer met her for the first time today after fifteen years, and yer say she's an angel?'

'I do.'

'Didn't take yer long to make up yer mind.'

'One glance at that divine face was enough.'

'She's pretty, of course.'

'You understate it. How in the space of a few brief years she can have succeeded in converting herself from the gargoyle of 1939 into the radiant, lovely, glamorous, superlative girl she is today simply beats me. It's the nearest thing to a miracle I ever struck. It just shows what can be done if you have the right spirit and the will to win.'

Lord Uffenham started. A sudden interest quickened his stare. The words he had just heard had been spoken, or he was dashed well mistaken, by the voice of love, and it seemed to him that this was a good thing and ought to be pushed along. Often he had dreamed wistfully of a Prince Charming who would some day pop up out of a trap and, if encouraged to play his cards right, take Jane's mind off Stanhope Twine before it was too late, and here, seated beside him, appeared to be the very man. He was about to probe and question, with a view to ascertaining the exact warmth of his companion's feelings, but at this moment Shipley Hall became visible through the trees, diverting his thoughts and sweeping him away on a wave of sentimentality.

Shipley Hall stood on a wide plateau, backed by rolling woodland, a massive white house set about with gay flower beds and spreading lawns. The sight of it, as the car turned in at the iron gates and rolled up the drive, drew from Lord Uffenham a low gurgle such as might have proceeded from the lips of his bulldog George on beholding a T-bone steak, and Bill, always sympathetic, knew how he was feeling. Some poignant stuff was written by the poet Thomas Moore in the nineteenth century descriptive of the emotions of the Peri who was excluded from Paradise, and those of the British landowner who is revisiting the old home which poverty has compelled him to let furnished to a rich American are virtually identical.

As if to underline and emphasize his state of exile, the Jaguar of the new owner was standing at the front door, and Lord

Uffenham eyed it askance. He had overcome his momentary weakness, and his long upper lip was stiff once more.

'That feller Bunyan's here,' he said.

'Yes, that's his car.'

'If we go in, he'll want to show yer round the place as if it belonged to him.'

Forbearing to twist the knife in the wound by pointing out that it did, Bill said:

'We'll have to go in, if I'm to look at those pictures.'

'Plenty of time for that. I want to show yer round myself. See that tree there? At the age of ten, concealed behind that tree, I once plugged an under-gardener in the seat of the pants with my bow and arrow. He was as sick as mud. See that rose garden?'

Bill saw the rose garden.

'Used to be a pond there. My niece fell into it when she was a kid, and just before she went down for the third time, was hauled out with leeches all over her.'

Bill's heart stood still. True, the incident had occurred a long time ago, and she was presumably all right now, but he shuddered to the foundations of his being at the picture of Jane submerged in the inky depths. There floated into his mind the passing thought that the woman he loved had apparently spent most of her formative years under water.

'Good God,' he cried, aghast.

'Sucking her blood like billy-o, they were. "Lord love a duck, Anne," I remember saying—'

'You mean Jane.'

'No, this wasn't Jane. It was her sister Anne.'

'Oh?' said Bill, immediately losing interest. He had no objection to leeches sucking blood – leeches will be leeches – provided they did not suck Jane's.

'I really ought to see those pictures,' he said. 'After all, it's what we came for.'

This seemed to strike Lord Uffenham, after some thought, as reasonable.

'Yerss, there's something in that, no doubt. All right, let's go in. What I'm hoping,' he said, as they made their way through paths with a history and shrubberies with a past, 'is that they'll fetch a whacking great sum and enable me to get back Shipley and push this Bunyan off the premises. Makes yer feel sort of at a loose end, getting kicked out of yer boyhood home. There have been Uffenhams at Shipley since I don't know how long. I suppose there's a lot of money in pictures?'

'You'd be surprised. Pop Gish has a Renoir he's expecting to sell for a hundred thousand dollars.'

'A hundred thousand dollars,' said Lord Uffenham, 'would be a great help. Here we are. We'll slip in at the side door. No need to stir up butlers and things.'

The picture gallery at Shipley Hall was on the first floor, reached by way of a polished and slippery oak staircase – ('Came a hell of a purler down these stairs at the age of fifteen, trying to avoid my Uncle Gregory, who was after me with a hunting crop for some reason which has escaped my memory') – and was occupied at the moment of their entry by Mortimer Bayliss. He eyed them frostily. He hated to be interrupted when looking at pictures.

'Hello, Mr Bayliss,' said Bill. 'A lovely afternoon, is it not?'

'Get out, you foul Hollister,' said Mortimer Bayliss in his cordial way. 'What do you think you're doing here?'

'In pursuance of my duties as Mr Gish's assistant, I've come to look at Lord Uffenham's pictures.'

'Oh? And who,' asked Mr Bayliss, indicating the sixth

Viscount, whom the poignant emotions caused by revisiting his old home had thrown into a trance, 'is your stuffed friend?'

'That's Lord Uffenham in person. He came along for the ride. Lord Uffenham!'

'Hey?'

'This is Mr Mortimer Bayliss, who is longing to meet you. He's an art expert.'

'What do you mean, *an* art expert?' said Mr Bayliss, piqued.

'Sorry. I should have said "the".'

'You certainly should, you beardless oaf.' Mr Bayliss turned his black-rimmed monocle on Lord Uffenham, scrutinizing him, it seemed to Bill, with a touch of pity. 'So you are the owner of these frightful daubs, are you?'

Bill started.

'Daubs?'

'No, I ought not to have called them that. Very good bits of work, some of them. But you realize, of course, that they're all forgeries?'

'What!'

'It might be a Roumanian art gallery. Somebody once said "If I were a forgery, where would I be?", and the answer was "In a Roumanian art gallery". Yes, they're fakes, every one of them.'

Lord Uffenham, who had been coming slowly out of his coma, emerged from it in time to hear these last words. He uttered an anguished 'Hey!'

'What was that you said? Fakes?'

'That was the gist of my remarks. I can tell you the artists' names, if you wish. This,' said Mr Bayliss, indicating the Gainsborough he had been examining, 'is undoubtedly a Wilfred Robinson. He painted a beautiful Gainsborough. That Constable is a Sidney Biffen. His middle period, I should say. About this Vermeer I'm not so sure. It might be a Paul Muller or it might be a Jan Dircks. Their style is somewhat similar, due no doubt to the fact that they were both pupils of Van Meegeren. Ah,' said Mr Bayliss with enthusiasm, 'there was a man, that Van Meegeren. Started out in a modest way forging De Hoochs, and then rose to Vermeers and never looked back. Sold the last one he did for half a million pounds. They don't make men like that nowadays. Still, Muller and Dircks are quite good, quite good. Not bad at all,' said Mr Bayliss tolerantly.

Lord Uffenham had the appearance of a man who has been struck by an unexpected thunderbolt. A faint 'Lord love a duck' escaped him.

'Yer mean the bally things aren't worth *anything*?'

'Oh, they'd fetch a few hundreds, I suppose, if you had the luck to find the right mug.' He looked at his watch. 'Hullo, as late as that? Time for my afternoon nap. Well, glad to have been of help,' said Mortimer Bayliss, and went out.

Bill, too, was feeling as if something hard and heavy had hit him. He had come to be very fond of Lord Uffenham, and it distressed him to see the stricken peer in his hour of travail. Lord Uffenham having reeled beneath the blow, had once more turned rigid, and was looking like a statue of himself subscribed for and erected by a few friends and admirers. Bill's heart bled for him.

It also bled for his employer. Mr Gish, he presumed, had been hoping for big things in the way of commission from the sale of these pictures. It would now be his, Bill's distasteful task to speak to him of Wilfred Robinson, of Sidney Biffen, of Paul Muller and Jan Dircks. With a compassionate glance at Lord Uffenham, who was still looking as if he had been hewn from the solid rock, he stole out, and a passing housemaid directed him to the telephone.

CHAPTER 13

Lord Uffenham was a resilient man. He might totter when thunderbolts hit him, but it was never long before he threw off their ill effects and returned to normal. Two minutes after Bill had left him, he was perking up. He had become aware that, though the storm clouds had unquestionably gathered, there was a silver lining in them. What had happened, he was feeling, might after all be for the best.

It would have been pleasant, of course, he mused, following this train of thought, to have made a packet out of the ancestral pictures, but you had to look at these things from every angle. When your niece has madly plighted her troth to a bally sculptor and needs only the slightest encouragement to go and get hitched up with him, making a packet has its disadvantages. If, reasoned Lord Uffenham, he had become a man of substance with money to give away in large handfuls, it would scarcely have been possible to deny the misguided girl her cut, and then what? Why, first thing you knew, some clergyman would have been saying to her 'Will yer, Jane, take this Stanhope?', and she would have been saying 'Well, Lord love a duck, that's the whole idea. What d'yer think I bought this wedding dress for?', and there she would have been, tied for life to the frightful feller. There were aspects of the activities of the Messrs Robinson, Biffen, Dircks and Muller at which one found oneself shaking the head a bit, but really, upon his soul, the clear-thinking peer told himself, things might have been a dashed sight worse.

It was consequently to a restored and revivified Lord Uffenham that Bill re-entered some ten minutes later. But as the other's rugged face seldom betrayed emotion of any sort, having much in common with that of a stuffed frog, his opening words were words of commiseration, the verbal equivalent of the silent hand-clasp and the sympathetic kneading of the shoulder blades.

'I'm awfully sorry,' he said, speaking like one who stands beside a sick-bed.

'Hey?'

'About the pictures.'

'Oh, those? Dismiss them from yer mind and don't give 'em a thought,' said Lord Uffenham buoyantly. 'Bit of a sock in the jaw at the moment, I admit, but a feller has to take the rough with the smooth. Easy come, easy go, is the way I look at it. One can see how it happened, of course. What yer've got to bear in mind is that I'm not the first Viscount by a long chalk. I'm the sixth. That means that there were five ruddy Viscounts before me, all needing the stuff and seeing those pictures standing there just waiting to be cashed in on. Here was a handy way of raising the wind, so they raised it, and very sensible, too. I should say my Uncle Gregory, the one I inherited from, probably dipped into the till more freely than any of them. He never had a bean, and as it was a sort of obsession with him to back horses that finished sixth, he always had all the bookies after him like a pack of wolves every settling-day. My old guv'nor used to say he wished he had a quid for every time he'd seen his brother Gregory running like the wind down Piccadilly with a high-up man from some turf accountant's firm in hot pursuit behind him. Kept him in wonderful condition, of course.'

Bill was relieved. He had not expected this fine spirit, so different from that exhibited by Mr Gish at their recent telephone conversation. Mr Gish, receiving the bad news, had mourned and would not be comforted.

'Well, I'm glad you take such a philosophical view.'

'Hey?'

'I was afraid you would be upset.'

'No use getting upset about these things. All in the day's work. But Jane isn't going to like it, I'm afraid. She was counting on those pictures to restore the family fortunes. I'd better go and 'phone her.'

'I'll come with you. I want to talk to Jane.'

'To express sympathy?'

'No, to ask her to marry me.'

'What an admirable idea! Lord love a duck! So I was right. You do love the wench?'

'I do.'

'Quick work.'

'That's the way we Hollisters are. We see, we love, we act, *Voilà!*'

'How d'yer mean, *Voilà?*'

'A French expression, signifying "There you have it in a nutshell". I must remember to tell Jane that. She thinks all the French I know is *"L'addition"* and *'Oo là là!"*.'

Standing beside the telephone while his companion rumbled on into it, Bill listened with growing impatience. Every minute that kept him from pouring out his soul to Jane was like an hour.

'So there y'are,' said Lord Uffenham, summing up. 'There yer have it in a nutshell. *Voilà!* . . . Hey? I said *Voilà!* A French expression. Don't be silly, my girl, of course you got it. V for vermicelli, O for—'

Bill could endure it no longer.

'Here, give me that telephone.'

'Oh, yerss, I was forgetting. Don't ring off, Jane. Here's some-one wants to talk to yer.'

Bill took the instrument, and Lord Uffenham whispered a word of warning.

'Pick yer words carefully, my boy, don't rush her.'

'I won't. Jane? Bill speaking. Look, Jane, this is important. Will you marry me?'

'That's what I meant by rushing her,' said Lord Uffenham, shaking his head reprovingly. 'Reminds me of a poem my old guv'nor used to read to me when I was a kid. About a feller named Alphonso and a wench called Emily. How did it go, now? Used to know it by heart once. Ah, yes, "Alphonso, who for cool assurance all creation licks, he up and said to Emily, who has cheek enough for six——" '

Bill had replaced the receiver. There was a rather stunned look on his face.

' "Miss Emily, I love yer. Will yer marry? Say the word", and Emily said "Certainly, Alphonso, like a bird".' He scanned Bill's face thoughtfully. 'I take it from something in yer manner that that wasn't what Jane said?'

'She didn't say anything. She gave a sort of gasp, and hung up.'

Lord Uffenham nodded sagely. In his younger days he had frequently heard girls gasp over the telephone, and it had always spelled trouble.

'I told yer not to rush her. See what's happened? You've made her ratty. She thought you were having a joke with her.'

'Having a joke?'

'Making fun of her. Pulling her leg. Well, what would *you* think if *you* were a girl, and a feller you hardly knew from a hole in the ground suddenly bellowed at yer "Hey! How about marrying me?"? No tact, no leading up to the thing gracefully, just "Hello there, let's get married", as if yer were inviting her out to tea and shrimps or something.'

How much more circumspectly, he was thinking, the Great Bustard would have comported itself in similar circumstances. The Great Bustard, as he had recently learned from his *Wonders Of The Bird World*, when entertaining for a female bustard feelings deeper and warmer than those of ordinary friendship, does not shout proposals of marriage over the telephone. It ruffles its back feathers, inflates its chest and buries its whiskers in it, thus showing tact and leading up to the thing gracefully. And he was about to pass these nature notes on to Bill, when the latter spoke. There was, Bill had realized, something in what the other had said.

'I was abrupt, you think?'

'That's how it struck me.'

Bill reflected.

'Yes, I suppose I was. It never occurred to me at the time.'

'Always a mistake, anyway, proposing on the telephone. I remember in the year 1920, when I was potty about a girl called Janice, ringing her up and saying "I love yer, I love yer. Will yer marry me?", and she said "You betcher. Of course I will".'

'Wasn't that all right?'

'Far from it. Because I'd got the numbers in my little red book mixed up, and it wasn't Janice I was talking to, it was a girl called Constance, whom I'd never much liked. Took me quite a while adjusting that situation.'

'Well, I've got to adjust this situation. Come on, let's get in that car and drive to your place. I'll have it out with her.'

'She won't be there. She'll have gone off to that school friend of hers, and you know how it is when girls from the old school get together. She may not be home till midnight.'

'But I must see her.'

'Come and have a bite of dinner tomorrow. Seven o'clock. Don't dress.'

Bill looked at Lord Uffenham with approval. The old gentleman might be an odd shape, but he got some good ideas.

'I will. Thank you very much.'

'I can promise yer an excellent dinner. Jane's a superb cook.'

'Does she cook?'

'Does she *cook*? Well, you ought to know. She did that dinner at Twine's that you were at last night. Good, wasn't it?'

'It was terrific. I was saying to somebody only this morning that it melted in the mouth. But what on earth was she doing cooking for Twine?'

'She's engaged to him.'

'Engaged? What do you mean?'

'What d'yer think I mean?'

'She's going to *marry* him?'

'So she says.'

It had sometimes happened to Bill, when indulging in his hobby of amateur boxing, to place the point of his jaw in a spot where his opponent was simultaneously placing his fist, and the result had always been a curious illusion that the top of his head had parted abruptly from its moorings. He experienced a similar sensation now. Tottering, he might have fallen, had he not clutched at something solid, which proved to be Lord Uffenham's arm. The latter uttered a yelp of the same nature as the one he had uttered in the garden of Peacehaven.

'Hey!'

Bill was still dazed.

'Oh, sorry,' he said. 'Did I grab you?'

'You grabbed me like a ton of bricks right in the fleshy part. Hurt like sin. What's the matter? Feeling faint?'

'No, I'm all right now. It gave me rather a shock for a moment.'

'I can well believe it. It gave *me* a shock, when she told me. When the wench breezed in one morning while I was doing my crossword puzzle and sprang it on me as calm as a halibut on ice that she was going to marry Stanhope Twine, I nearly swooned where I sat. "What!" I said. "*That* young slab of damnation? Yer kiddin." But no. She stuck to it that it was all fixed up. Stuck stoutly.'

Bill stood plunged in thought, and Lord Uffenham heaved a sigh.

'I don't mind telling you that the whole thing has come very near to breaking my ruddy heart. *Twine*, I'll trouble yer!'

'I know what you mean.'

'A feller who marcels his hair.'

'Yes.'

'And wears yellow corduroy trousers.'

'Yes.'

'The last chap in the world one wants about the house.'

'I quite agree with you. We can't have this sort of thing going on. We must put a stop to it at once.'

'But how?'

'I shall talk to her and make her see the light.'

'You won't rush her?'

'Certainly not. I shall be very calm and tactful and persuasive. I know just the tone to take.'

'You think you'll be able to prise her away from him?'

'I think so.'

'Well, best of luck, my dear boy. If you do, nobody will wave his hat and cheer more heartily than I. But I don't mind telling yer that so far the voice of reason has been powerless to drive sense into her fat head. Lord love a duck,' said Lord Uffenham, heaving another sigh, 'when I think of Jane wanting to marry Stanhope Twine and remember that her sister Anne came within an ace of marrying an interior decorator, I ask myself if there may not be a touch of eccentricity in the family.'

On the rare occasions when the weather was fine enough to permit of it, it was Roscoe Bunyan's custom to take his before-dinner cocktail on the terrace opening off the drawing-room of Shipley Hall, from which one got a charming view of rolling parkland and distant woods, and it was here on the evening following the visit of Bill and Lord Uffenham to Shipley that he might have been observed giving a rather close imitation of an expectant father at a maternity home – sitting down, jumping up, pacing to and fro and generally behaving with the uneasy mobility usually associated with peas on shovels and cats on hot bricks. That morning Mortimer Bayliss had gone off to give Stanhope Twine lunch at his club and place the twenty-thousand-pound proposition before him, and at any moment now he would be returning from his mission, bringing the news of its success or failure.

That Roscoe, at first so reluctant to part with this substantial sum, should now be all of a twitter lest at the eleventh hour something should have gone wrong with the negotiations, preventing him from doing so, may seem peculiar. But in the period that had elapsed since the departure of Keggs the business sense which he had inherited from his father, the late J. J., had had time to work, and it had told him that, however keen the agony of bidding farewell to twenty thousand pounds, if he paid it out and in return secured a million dollars, he would be left with a most attractive profit. And attractive profits were meat and drink to him.

Presently Skidmore arrived with the cocktails, but it was only after his employer had had one quick and was starting on another rather slower that Mortimer Bayliss appeared, looking like an Egyptian mummy in need of a bracer.

'At last!' cried Roscoe.

Mr Bayliss headed purposefully for the cocktail table, though only in quest of tomato juice. It was many years since his medical adviser had prohibited anything more in tune with modern enlightened thought. Like Jamshyd, the curator of the Bunyan Collection had once gloried and drunk deep, but those brave old days were over.

'Were you expecting me earlier?' he said, sipping the hell-brew and wishing, as he so often wished, that it tasted a little less like a weak solution of old galoshes. 'I looked in at the Gish Galleries after lunch. It always amazes me that Leonard Gish is still a free man. I'd have thought that he would long since have been doing his bit of time at Wormwood Scrubbs or Pentonville. Negligence somewhere.'

Roscoe was in no mood to discuss Mr Gish.

'What happened?' he asked, quivering.

'He tried to get two hundred thousand dollars out of me for that Renoir of his. Worth at the most a hundred thousand. That's an art dealer for you.'

Roscoe continued to impersonate a tuning fork. 'At lunch, man! What happened at your lunch with Twine?'

'Oh, that? Everything went according to plan. I gave him your cheque, and he rushed off, without waiting for coffee, to deposit it.'

Roscoe collapsed into a chair with a grunt of relief.

'I was afraid he might back out.'

'There was never any chance of that. For a moment I thought he was going to kiss me. Sometimes,' said Mortimer Bayliss, gazing with distaste at his tomato juice, 'I am tempted to rebel, to tell these doctors where they can stick their medical advice and go back to the spacious times when I was known as Six-Martini Bayliss. Then I tell myself that it is not fair on the world to deprive it of its finest art expert. Yes, as of course one knew he would, Twine jumped at it.

'Swell!'

Mortimer Bayliss removed his monocle, polished it thoughtfully, replaced it in his eye and through it gazed at his companion in a way that would have struck a beholder more sensitive to impressions than Roscoe as enigmatic.

'Swell?' he said meditatively. 'I wonder—'

'What do you mean?'

'I am not wholly convinced that everything is as rosy as you seem to imagine.'

A disturbing thought struck Roscoe.

'Don't tell me he's not engaged?'

'He's engaged all right.'

'Well, then?'

Mortimer Bayliss finished his tomato juice, put the glass on the table, shuddered a little and said that the Borgias could have learned a lot, if they had lived today.

'Yes, he told me he was engaged, but something else he happened to mention made me ask myself if you are quite as much on velvet as I am sure we should all like you to be. He was touching on the parental opposition to his artistic career. His father disliked the idea of him becoming a sculptor, he told me. I wasn't surprised. These hay, corn and feed merchants always want their sons to go into the business.'

Roscoe could not follow this.

'These what?'

'Twine's father is a prosperous hay, corn and feed man up in Liverpool. Twine and Bessemer is, I understand, the name of the firm.'

Roscoe's bewilderment deepened.

'But he's an American.'

'Twine? No, English. No connection with America at all.'

'Keggs said—'

Mortimer Bayliss's face still had the impassivity of something that had died on the banks of the Nile five thousand years ago, but inwardly he was bubbling with merriment. He had no liking for the Roscoes of this world.

'Ah, that brings me to what I have been trying to break gently to you, my dear boy. What Keggs says, when he comes and hands you a million dollars on a plate with watercress round it and you reward him with a measly fifty pounds, is not evidence. His haughty spirit wounded, he told you Twine was the man, knowing well that Twine was not the man, thus getting his own back by making you pay twenty thousand pounds for nothing. From what I know of Keggs, and I used to study him rather closely in the old days, that sort of thing would appeal to his peculiar sense of humour. I don't want to rub it in, but I must say I have often felt that your thriftiness would get you into trouble some day.'

The rolling parkland and the distant woods were flickering before Roscoe's eyes like an early silent motion picture. He rose, his face purple and his eyes gleaming.

'I'll wring the man's neck.'

'Well, if you must, of course. But there's a law against it.'

'I'll go and do it now.'

'How about dinner?'

'I don't want any dinner.'

'I do,' said Mortimer Bayliss. 'I need it sorely. But I can't miss seeing you wring Keggs's neck. I'll come with you. I'm one of those modern teen-agers you read about – avid for excitement.'

It was not often that Lord Uffenham entertained guests at his Mulberry Grove residence, for he preferred, when exercising hospitality, to do it at his club. But when he did so entertain, it was Augustus Keggs's kindly practice to buckle on his discarded armour, as he had done on the night of Stanhope Twine's dinner party, and leap into the breach, buttling as devotedly as in the old Shipley Hall days. Augustus Keggs, though retired and a capitalist, was still animated by the feudal spirit.

It was he, in consequence, who opened the front door of Castlewood to Bill on his arrival, and the latter, who had been subjected to a considerable strain these last few days, had a momentary feeling that he had cracked under it and was seeing things. Then a plausible solution suggested itself. Keggs, he decided, must be a specialist who, in return for some suitable fee, hired himself out for the evening when Valley Fields felt like making whoopee. He greeted him with the cordiality of an old friend.

'Hello,' he said, 'we're seeing a lot of each other these days, aren't we?'

'Yes, indeed, sir,' Keggs agreed, smiling indulgently.

'You seem to pop from spot to spot like the chamois of the

Alps leaping from crag to crag. I don't believe I gave you my name last time, did I? Well, there must be no secrets and reservations between old buddies like us. It's Hollister.'

Respectful interest came into Keggs's gooseberry eyes.

'Indeed, sir? Might I enquire, if it is not a liberty, if you are the son of Mr Joseph Hollister, formerly of New York City?'

'Yes, that's right. My father's name was Joseph. You knew him?'

'I was in the service of the late Mr J. J. Bunyan many years ago, and Mr Hollister senior was a frequent dinner guest at our table. I was struck immediately by the resemblance. If you will step this way, sir. His lordship is in his study.'

The study was a large, airy room, comfortably furnished in country-house style, for Lord Uffenham on being driven from his garden of Eden had been at pains to loot the place of all the chairs, rugs, pictures, books and personal belongings he liked best. On the walls hung photographs of him at every stage of his development . . . the schoolboy, the undergraduate, the guards- man, the boulevardier and the warrior of the battlefields of Loos and the Somme . . . and it would have interested Bill to examine these, to see if his host had always been that peculiar shape. But he was given no opportunity of doing so, for Lord Uffenham, who was looking grave as though he had recently received disturbing news, thrust him into a chair, handed him a cocktail and immediately began to speak.

'Holloway,' he said.

Bill mentioned that the name was Hollister, and Lord Uffen- ham said Oh was it, adding that the point was immaterial, for now that they had become such close friends, he proposed to address him as Augustus.

'Why?' asked Bill, interested.

'It's yer name.'

'My name is not Augustus.'

'*Not* Augustus?'

'No, not Augustus.'

Lord Uffenham clicked his tongue.

'I see where I went wrong. Keggs's name is Augustus. That's what muddled me. I don't always get names right. My niece Anne, Jane's sister—'

'The one who fell into the pond?'

'That's right, and got leeches all over her. She got spliced to a young feller called Jeff Miller, and it was only after a considerable lapse of time that I was able to rid myself of the belief that his name was Walter Willard.'

'I don't call that such a bad shot.'

'No. But one likes to be accurate. Jane's always on at me about it.'

'Where is Jane?'

'In the kitchen.'

'Should I go and have a word with her?'

'I wouldn't advise it. Women hate to be interrupted when dishing up dinner, especially if already ratty. Yerss, Fred, she's still ratty, I'm sorry to say. Goes about in a sort of dream, looking like a dying duck, and doesn't answer when you speak to her. She's in shock.'

'Oh, no, really.'

'In shock,' repeated Lord Uffenham firmly. 'And why wouldn't she be, after the way you rushed her? Why, there was a girl I used to know in 1912 who got in shock once because I didn't like her new hat. Took a diamond sunburst to bring her round, I remember. You shook Jane to her bally foundations, my boy, and if you're going to make her cast off the spell of the hell-hound

Twine, you'll have to spit on yer hands and pull your socks up in no uncertain manner. Because a very serious situation has arisen. You know what she told me this evening just before going off to put the chicken in the oven? She told me that Twine has got his hooks on a whacking great sum of money.'

Bill started.

'Twine has? How much?'

'Twenty thousand ruddy pounds. No less.'

'What!'

'It's a fact. She had it direct from Keggs, who appears to have been present throughout the whole conversation between Bunyan and that art expert chap.'

'Bayliss?'

'I'd have said Banstead.'

'But what have he and Bunyan to do with it?'

'I'm telling yer. It seems that the feller Bunyan and the feller Banstead were talking about the feller Twine's statues, and the feller Banstead said the feller Twine was a genius or words to that effect; and the upshot of the whole thing is that Bunyan's given Twine twenty thousand pounds in return for a percentage of his future earnings. Must have been as tight as an owl, I should say, but there it is. So Twine, blister his insides, now has twenty thousand of the best in his hip pocket. You see what this means? It means that the only shield and safeguard we had against him marrying Jane – the fact that he couldn't afford to – no longer exists. He could marry fifty Janes. If,' said Lord Uffenham, having reviewed this statement, 'he were a Mormon. Not otherwise, of course. Yerss,' he concluded, 'that frightful young blot on the landscape has now got the stuff, and if you're going to accomplish anything constructive, Fred, yer'll have to look slippy.'

His gravity had communicated itself to Bill. Until now, he had been inclined, even though Jane was engaged to him, to under-estimate Stanhope Twine as a menace. But a Stanhope Twine whose corduroy trousers were bulging with Roscoe Bunyan's gold might well be a formidable rival. Unquestionably socks would have to be pulled up and hands spat on, not to mention stones turned and avenues explored.

'You're sure of this?' he said.

'I tell yer, Keggs was there.'

'Where?'

'At Shipley, where the conversation took place.'

'What was he doing there?'

'He'd gone to see Bunyan about something.'

'Odd them discussing a thing like that in front of Keggs.'

'He was probably listening at the keyhole.'

'And another thing I don't understand is how Roscoe could ever have brought himself to risk twenty thousand pounds on the future of an unknown man. It doesn't sound like him.'

Lord Uffenham saw that his young friend had got mixed up. He was quite patient about it. He knew that he sometimes got mixed up himself.

'It was not Roscoe. It was Bunyan.'

'His name is Roscoe.'

'No, it's not. It's Bunyan.'

'His Christian name.'

Enlightenment flooded on Lord Uffenham. He could be as quick as lightning at times.

'Oh, his *Christian* name? Now I've got yer. Now I follow yer.'

'The thing seems absolutely incredible. Roscoe never parts. He's noted for it. He is known far and wide as the man with the one-way pockets.'

Lord Uffenham was beginning to feel a little impatient. He spoke with some sharpness.

'Well, he's parted now.'

'If the story's true.'

'Of course it's true. Why would Keggs invent a yarn like that? You're wandering from the point, Fred. We mustn't waste precious time asking ourselves *why* Ronald Bunyan committed this rash act. We've got to put our heads together and decide what's to be done. Have another cocktail?'

'Thanks. I feel I need one.'

'Two problems confront us,' said Lord Uffenham, having refilled their glasses: '(*a*) how to stop Jane being ratty with yer, and (*b*) how to prevent her charging off to the registrar's and getting spliced to the Twine excrescence. The first is the tricky one. Solve that, and you'll be in a position to handle Problem B for yerself. Because you aren't going to tell me you're not capable of cutting out a blister like Stanhope Twine. And you'll be relieved to hear, Fred, that I have the matter well in hand.'

'You have?'

'Yerss, I see the way. We can get cracking. You ever read poetry?'

'Quite a good deal. Why?'

'I was thinking that once in a while those poets stumble on something that makes sense. Remember the feller who said that women were gosh-awful pains in the neck when things were going right with you, but turned into bally angels when yer had a hangover?'

'"Oh, woman, in our hours of ease . . ."'

'That's the one. My old guv'nor used to recite it whenever he got a bit bottled. Well, there's a lot in it. Take Jane. At the moment ratty, but if pain and anguish were to wring yer brow, she'd be all over yer, I'm convinced of it. It was the same with her sister Anne.'

'The one who married Walter Willard?'

Lord Uffenham tut-tutted.

'You want to watch yerself over names, Fred,' he said rebukingly. 'Miller I told yer he was called, Jeff Miller. Your trouble is yer don't retain. Yerss, Jeff Miller, a fine young chap whom I looked on as a son, loved my niece Anne and kept pressing his suit; but the cloth-headed girl would have none of him, being under the extraordinary illusion that what she wanted was a putty-souled interior decorator named Lionel Green. When Jeff wooed her, it made her as sore as a gumboil. She wouldn't speak to him, and she had developed a habit, when they found themselves alone together, of whizzing from his presence as if shot from a gun. This made things difficult for Jeff.'

'It must have done. Complex, you might say?'

'Very complex. He began to lose heart, feeling that he was making no solid progress. All this, I should mention, was taking place down at Shipley under my personal eye, and I don't mind telling yer that my flesh used to creep when I saw Anne giving Jeff the sleeve across the windpipe and realized that every minute brought closer the day when she would become the bride of this pestilential poop Lionel Green. I could see no hope of easing the tension and finding a formula, and I was trying to steel myself to the prospect of becoming the uncle of an interior decorator, when one evening by the greatest good luck a sweet little woman named Mrs Molloy, who was staying at Shipley at the time, hauled off and walloped Jeff over the head with my tobacco jar.'

It seemed to Bill that the home life of his host presented what Sherlock Holmes would have called certain features of interest.

'She did?'

'Bang on the occipital bone. It's a long story. She and her husband were crooks, and Jeff caught them trying to loot the house. He started hammering the stuffing out of Molloy, so Mrs Molloy very naturally crowned him with the tobacco jar. And that, of course, made everything all right between him and Anne.'

'All right?' Bill was conscious of a feeling, such as comes to all of us at times, of not being equal to the intellectual pressure of the conversation. 'Why?'

'Hey?'

'Why was that the happy ending?'

'Because it opened Anne's eyes. It made her look into her heart and read its message. Seeing Jeff lying there with his toes turned up and giving every evidence of having handed in his dinner pail, she knew in a flash that he was the one she loved, and she flung herself on his prostrate form and started to kiss him, at the same time saying "Oh, Jeff, darling", and all that sort of thing. Never gave Lionel Green another thought. Interesting story. Throws a light on feminine psychology.'

'It must have been a solid tobacco jar.'

'It was. I bought it when I went up to Cambridge. When you're a freshman, the first thing yer buy is a stone tobacco jar with the college arms on it. I'll show it to yer,' said Lord Uffenham, lumbering across the room and returning with the blunt instrument. 'Good value there,' he said, regarding it affectionately. 'Forty-odd years I've had it, and still unbroken. Jeff's head didn't even dent it. Lord love a duck, I can see the scene as plainly as if it had happened yesterday. There was Jeff squaring away at Molloy – unpleasant feller, he was. Going a bit bald on the top, I remember – and Mrs Molloy – Dolly her name was, and, as I say, a sweet little woman, though of course with some defects – upped with the jar and let him have it. Like this,' said

Lord Uffenham, and lumbered to the door. 'Jane,' he called. 'Jay-un.'

'Yes?'

'Cummere. Young Holloway's had an accident. I was showing him that tobacco jar of mine, and my hand slipped.'

It was some little time later that Bill, waking from a disordered nightmare in which strange and violent things had been happening to him, became aware that someone was standing at his side, offering him a glass of brandy.

'Take a sip of this, my boy,' said Lord Uffenham, for it was he. The altruistic peer was wearing a look of smug satisfaction such as some great general might have worn after a famous victory. Wellington probably looked like that at Waterloo.

Bill took a sip, and found his head clearing. He fixed a bleary and accusing eye on his host.

'Was that you?' he said coldly.

'Hey?'

'Did you hit me with that tobacco jar?'

The smug expression on Lord Uffenham's face was rendered more repellent by a modest smirk. He seemed to be deprecating thanks. It was as though he were saying that it was nothing, nothing, that any man would have done what he had done.

'Yerss, that's right. Bring the young folks together, that's what I say. As I had anticipated, it worked. I take it you weren't noticing much at the time, so I'll give yer a brief outline of what occurred. I went to the door, shouted "Jane! Jay-un!" and she shouted back "What the hell's the matter now?" or words to that effect, no doubt being busy with the dinner and not wanting to have her mind taken off it. "Cummere," I said. "Young Holloway's had an accident." And up she comes and, seeing your prostrate form, flings herself on it and kisses yer. The usual routine.'

Bill had not supposed that any human power would have been able to do anything to diminish the throbbing ache in a head which was feeling as if something of about the dimensions of Stanhope Twine's colossal nude had fallen on it from a seventh floor window, but at these words the throbbing ceased to be, the ache was no more. In their place came a yeasty elation such as he had never experienced, not even when reading the letter from Miss Angela Murphrey, freeing him of his honourable obligation. He felt like the uplifted gentleman in the poem who on honeydew had fed and drunk the milk of Paradise, and would not have been greatly surprised had Lord Uffenham said 'Beware, beware! His flashing eyes, his floating hair!' and woven a circle round him thrice.

He drew one of those deep breaths which lately had become such a feature of his existence.

'She kissed me?' he said reverently.

'Like nobody's business. At the same time crying "Oh, Bill, darling! Speak to me, Bill, darling! Lord love a duck, are yer dead, Bill, darling?" and so on and so forth. Odd that she should have called yer Bill, when yer name's Fred, but that's a side issue and probably without importance. The point to keep steadily before us is that she said "Darling" and kissed yer. Weighing the evidence, Fred, I think we can say the thing's in the bag.'

Bill rose and began to pace the room. Curiously, considering on how dashing, one might almost say fiery, lines his wooing had been conducted, his chief emotion, apart from that feeling of ecstasy which made him want to slap all mankind on the back, starting with Lord Uffenham, was a deep humility. He was weighed down with a sense of unworthiness, much as a swine-herd in a fairy tale might have been, who found himself loved by the princess. How his personality could have cast such a spell he was unable to understand.

It was not as though he had been a sort of Greek god or movie star. There was a mirror over the fireplace in Lord Uffenham's study, and he paused for a moment to examine himself in it. It was just as he had supposed. An honest face, but nothing more. One formed a picture of Jane Benedick as one of those exceptional girls who do not go by the outer crust but burrow through till they have found the soul within.

Yet even this explanation scarcely held water. His soul, as he knew, having lived a lifetime with it, was a good enough soul, as souls went, but not by any means the kind you hang out flags about. It was probably entered in the celestial books as 'Soul, gent's ordinary, one'. But despite all this she had flung herself on his prostrate form and kissed him, at the same time saying 'Oh, Bill, darling! Speak to me, Bill, darling! Lord love a duck, are yer dead, Bill, darling?' It was all very mystifying, and if the story had not proceeded from a reliable source, his informant having been an actual eye-witness, he could hardly have believed it.

An intense desire to see her swept over him.

'Where is she?' he cried.

'She stepped out to get some cold water and a sponge, and,' said Lord Uffenham, starting visibly, 'I hear her coming back. I'll be moving along, I think.'

Jane entered, bearing a basin, and as she saw the head of the family her eyes flashed fire.

'Uncle George,' she said, speaking from between clenched teeth.

'Quite. Quite. But got one or two things to attend to just now, my dear. See yer later,' said Lord Uffenham, and disappeared like a diving duck.

Jane put the basin down. The fire had died from her eyes, and they were moist.

'Oh, Bill!' she said.

He could not speak. Words – and this was a thing that rarely happened where he was concerned – failed him. He could but look at her in silence, wondering anew how this golden princess had ever brought herself to stoop to a man like himself – just one of the swineherds, as you might say, and not much of a swineherd at that. How lovely she was, he was thinking, though in forming this view he was in actual fact mistaken. A girl cannot stand over a kitchen stove on a warm June night, cooking a chicken and two veg., not to mention clear soup, and other delicacies, and remain natty. Jane's face was flushed and her hair dishevelled, and across one cheek there was a smudge of what appeared to be blacklead. Nevertheless, she seemed to him perfection. This, he told himself sentimentally, was how he must always remember her – with a grubby face and an apron round her waist.

'Jane!' he whispered. 'Oh, Jane!'

'This,' said Jane some moments later, 'can't be doing your head good.'

'It's doing *me* good,' Bill assured her. 'For the first time I'm beginning to realize that there may be something in this, that I'm not just dreaming. Or am I?'

'No.'

'You really—?'

'Of course I do. You're my Bill.'

'Once again Bill became conscious of that respiratory embarrassment and the absence of endotracheal oxygenation. He shrugged his shoulders, giving the thing up. But his soul was singing, and his heart was light.

'Well, it all seems most peculiar to me, you being what you are and I being what I am. I ask myself "What have you done to deserve this, William Quackenbush Hollister?" . . .'

'William *what* Hollister?'

'Not my fault, my godfather's. Don't let it put you off me. Think of me as Q. What, I was saying, have I done to deserve this? and the answer, as far as I have been able to work it out, is "Not a damn thing". Still, if you say so . . . What are you doing with that sponge?'

'I'm going to bathe your head.'

'Good God, this is no time for bathing heads. I want to tell you, if I can find words, how I feel about you. You're wonderful!'

'No, no. I'm just a simple little home body.'

'You are *not*. You're lovely.'

'You didn't always think so, did you?'

'You mean when we were tots? I was but a boy then, incapable of spotting a good thing when I saw one. Tell me, by the way, about this loveliness of yours. When did you feel it coming on?'

'I believe I began to look fairly human when I was about fourteen. They had removed the telephone switchboard effects by then.'

'And the spectacles?'

'And the spectacles. The strabismus had been corrected.'

Bill heaved a sigh, thinking of all he had missed through not having seen her at the age of fourteen. They were sitting now in Lord Uffenham's armchair, a roomy affair well adapted to the reception of two young people who did not mind being fairly close together. From the wall above them a photograph of Lord Uffenham in some sort of Masonic uniform gazed down

– benevolently, it seemed, as if he were saying 'Bless yer, my children'.

'When you were fourteen, I must have been slogging through Normandy on my way to Paris with the army of liberation.'

'Shouting "*Oo là là*"?'

'That and '*l'addition*'. Everybody said I was a great help. Don't wriggle.'

'I'm not wriggling, I'm getting up. I'm going to bathe your head.'

'I don't want my head bathed.'

'But you've got an enormous lump.'

'I ignore it. These things cannot affect us finally. I'm glad, though, that this didn't happen when my Lord Uffenham was younger and stronger.'

The cold, stern look returned to Jane's face.

'Don't mention that man's name in my presence. He ought to be in Colney Hatch.'

'Nonsense. I won't hear a word against Uncle George. He moves in a mysterious way, his wonders to perform, but he gets results. He brought the young folks together.'

'Nevertheless, he ought to be skinned – very slowly – with a blunt knife and dipped in boiling oil. That would teach him. I do wish that the men who marry into our family didn't always have to be hit over the head with that tobacco jar.'

'Have you no respect for tradition? But I see what you mean. One of these days, you feel, some suitor with a thin skull is going to land the old philanthropist in the dock on a murder charge.'

'There won't be any more suitors, because there aren't any more Benedicks. It's like Uncle George's rabbits. The supply has given out.'

'Well, I've got the Benedick *I* want.'

'You ought to have seen the one that got away.'

'Anne.'

'Ah yes, your plain sister.'

'She isn't. She's the prettiest thing you ever saw.'

Bill could not yield on this point.

'Any sister of yours – even if she were Cleopatra and Lillian Russell and Marilyn Munroe rolled into one – would be your plain sister. Anyway, I doubt if Anne would have appealed to me. All those leeches. Tell me, to settle a bet, is she Mrs Jeff Miller or Mrs Walter Willard?'

'The former.'

'Had Jeff Miller known her long?'

'No.'

'Then I am one up on him there. I am marrying my childhood sweetheart. Much more romantic.'

'Childhood sweetheart? I like that. When we were at Meadowhampton, you never gave me a look.'

'We went into all that. You were a gargoyle.'

'So when you say you love me, it is for my looks alone?'

'It is not for your damed looks alone. We'd better get this straight before proceeding further. I'm marrying you for your cooking, and I shall keep a very sharp look-out for any falling off from the standard. And if we're digging up the dead past, what about you and Twine? Yes, I don't wonder you hang your head and shuffle your feet. I take my eye off you for half a minute—'

'Fifteen years.'

'I take my eye off you for a mere fifteen years, and what happens? You leave me flat for a fellow who wears yellow corduroy trousers. And that brings me to a rather important item on the agenda paper. What do we do about Twine? He should be informed, I think. Scarcely humane to keep him in the dark till he gets his slice of wedding cake. What steps do we take?'

'Oh, Bill!'

'What's the matter? You're crying.'

'No, I'm laughing.'

'What's so funny?'

'Your saying about taking steps. We don't need to take any steps. He's taken them.'

Bill stared.

'You mean he's given you the push?'

'He called it releasing me.'

'Tell me all.'

'There isn't much to tell. I thought his manner seemed a little strange this morning, when I was breaking it to him that there would be no money coming in from those pictures, and this evening, just before you arrived, I had a note from him. It was a beautiful note. He said he felt he had no right to—'

'Don't tell me. Let me guess. Take the best years of your life?'

'Yes. He said it was wrong to hold me to my promise when there was so little chance of his ever having enough money to marry on, so he thought it only fair to release me. It was touching.'

'Doesn't he call twenty-thousand pounds enough money?'

'He didn't know I knew about that.'

'No, I imagine not.'

'I can see how his mind worked. Did you ever hear the story about the man in the first war who enlisted in the infantry instead of the cavalry because—'

' "When Ah run away, Ah don't aim to be hampered by no

horse." Yes, Mortimer Bayliss told me that one in one of his rare jovial moments, when I was a boy. How does it apply?'

'Well, Stanhope was always talking about how he ought to be travelling in Italy and France and all that, to broaden his mind and improve his art, and now that he's able to travel, he don't aim to be hampered by no wife. Especially a wife without any money. He's rather a self-centred man.'

'What did you ever see in him, you misguided little half-wit?'

'I suppose Uncle George's theory is the right one, though I wouldn't tell him so, it's bad for discipline. "Yer wouldn't have looked twice at the feller", he said, "if yer hadn't been cooped up in a London suburb with nobody else in sight." That must have been it. You get talking across the fence, and one thing leads to another.'

'And those yellow trousers probably dazzled you. Well, all right, I'll overlook it this time, but don't let it occur again.' Bill paused, listening. 'Do you keep an elephant here?'

'Not that I know of. Though Uncle George has often talked of buying an ostrich, if the funds will run to it. He wants to see if it will really bury its head in the sand. Why do you ask?'

'I thought I heard one coming up the stairs.'

It was not an elephant, it was the sixth Viscount Uffenham. He burst into the room, looking – for him – quite animated.

'Hey!' he said. 'What's going on in that ruddy kitchen? Smoke's billowing out of it in clouds, and it smells to heaven.'

Jane uttered a stricken cry.

'Oh, death and despair, the dinner! It must be burned to a cinder.'

She darted out, and Lord Uffenham followed her with an indulgent eye.

'Women!' he said, with a short, amused laugh. 'Well, Fred, how did things work out?'

'Fine, Uncle George. You are losing a niece, but gaining a nephew.'

'Excellent. Couldn't be better.'

'Well, actually, it could be a lot better, because I'm really much too poor to think of getting married. All I have is my pittance from the Gish Galleries.'

'Nothing else?'

'Not a cent.'

'Pity those pictures turned blue on us.'

'Yes, but you've got to weigh this against that. If it hadn't been for them, I should never have met Jane.'

'That's true. Oh, well, something'll turn up. Yes, Keggs?'

Keggs had floated in, looking grave.

'Miss Benedick desired me to step up and inform your Lordship that she regrets that it will be impossible for her to provide dinner tonight,' he said in a hushed voice.

Lord Uffenham waved dinner away with an airy gesture.

'Gone west, has it? Well, who cares? Keggs, I want yer to fill a glass and drink the health of the young couple.'

'M'lord?'

'Young Fred Holloway here and my niece Jane. They're getting spliced.'

'Indeed, m'lord? I am sure I wish you every happiness, sir.'

Jane came in. She was dirty and dispirited.

'There won't be any dinner,' she said. 'It's a charred ruin. We'll have to go to that pub you and Mr Keggs sneak off to in the evenings.'

Lord Uffenham scoffed at this pedestrian suggestion.

'What?' he cried. 'Go to the local on a night like this, when

yer've seen the light and given that perisher Twine the heave-
ho, and hitched on to a splendid young feller whom I can nurse
in my bosom? Not by a jugful. We'll go to Barribault's, and you'd
better wash yer face, my girl. It's a mass of smuts. Makes yer
look as if yer'd blacked up to sing comic songs with a banjo from
a punt at Henley Regatta.'

The discovery that a wolf in butler's clothing has with subtle chicanery tricked him out of twenty thousand pounds always affects the precision of a motorist's driving, and this is especially so if he is a motorist who sets as high a value on money as did Roscoe Bunyan. It was not long after setting out for Valley Fields that Roscoe, his thoughts elsewhere, ran his Jaguar into a telegraph pole, inflicting it with internal injuries so severe that he had to walk back to Shipley Hall and get the station wagon. It was consequently somewhat late when he and Mortimer Bayliss arrived at Castlewood and were admitted by Augustus Keggs.

Keggs showed no surprise at seeing them. It had occurred to him that he might shortly be receiving a visit from the son of his old employer. He admired and respected Mortimer Bayliss, but he knew him to be a man incapable of keeping a good joke to himself. The incursion of the Shipley Hall party found him, therefore, prepared, and he was all amiability and old-world courtesy, in sharp contradistinction to Roscoe, who resembled a volcano about to spread molten lava over the countryside while thousands flee. He conducted the visitors to his cosy sitting-room, and put a green baize cloth over the canary's cage, so as to ensure an absence of background music, always so disturbing at anything in the nature of a board meeting. Nobody could have been more suave. Even when Roscoe, finding speech, called him six deleterious names, the mildest of which was 'fat swindler', he continued to look like a particularly saintly bishop.

'I had anticipated a certain show of displeasure on your part, sir,' he said equably, 'but I am sure Mr Bayliss will agree with me that nothing is to be gained by recrimination.'

Mortimer Bayliss was in edgy mood. He resented being snatched away from the dinner to which he had been looking forward for several hours. He regarded Roscoe sourly, thinking, as he so often thought, what a degenerate scion he was of old J. J., whom in spite of numerous faults he had rather liked. J. J. Bunyan had been an old pirate, and his business ethics had often made the judicious grieve, but there had been a spaciousness about him reminiscent of some breezy buccaneer of the Spanish Main. There was nothing spacious about Roscoe. He was, in Mortimer Bayliss's opinion, a mean-souled young twerp.

'Quite right,' he snapped. 'This is a business conference.'

Roscoe quivered in every chin.

'You expect me to be polite to the oily old thug after he's pulled a fast one like that?'

'You can't blame him for getting a bit of his own back. I told you you would be sorry for trying to fob him off with a measly fifty pounds. It hurt his feelings.'

'It did indeed, sir,' said Keggs, looking reproachfully at Roscoe, like a bishop who has found his favourite curate smoking marihuana. 'Fifty pounds in return for all that I was doing for you, sir. It wounded me deeply.'

'Well, now you've wounded *him* deeply, so you're all square and can start again from scratch. And for heaven's sake,' said Mortimer Bayliss, 'let's get a move on, because I want my dinner.

I take it that you are now prepared to reveal the real name of the mystery man who is his fellow-survivor in the Bayliss Matrimonial Tontine?'

Here Mr Bayliss thought it advisable to give Augustus Keggs a long, steady look, a look that said as plain as whisper in the ear 'Tell him you told me, and I'll strangle you with my bare hands'. Much as he enjoyed baiting Roscoe, the nature of their relations made it injudicious to alienate him beyond hope of forgiveness, as must inevitably happen, were that thrifty young man to learn that a word from him, Bayliss, would have saved him twenty thousand pounds and that that word had not been spoken. Roscoe, whatever his shortcomings as a human being, was the owner of the Bunyan Collection and, as such, in a position to dispense with the services of its curator.

Keggs, already shown in this chronicle as an expert diagnostician of starts and snorts, was equally competent as an interpreter of long, steady looks. He had no difficulty in reading the message that was flashing from the black-rimmed monocle. If he had been a shade less dignified, one might have described the quick, slight flutter which disturbed his left eyelid as a wink.

'Certainly, sir,' he said, 'if suitable terms can be arranged.'

'What's your idea of suitable terms?'

'A hundred thousand dollars, sir.'

Roscoe had already drained the bitter cup so deeply that one might have supposed that an extra sip would not have affected him very much, but these words brought him out of his chair as if, in Lord Uffenham's powerful phrase, shot from a gun. His appearance and manner were those of a short-tempered whale which has just received a harpoon in a tender spot.

'What! Why, you—'

'Please, sir!' said Keggs.

'Please, Roscoe!' said Mortimer Bayliss. 'We shall get nowhere, if you start interrupting. A hundred thousand dollars, you think, Keggs? Cash down?'

'Oh, no, sir. What I had in mind was five thousand pounds in advance and the remainder when the proceeds of the tontine are in Mr Roscoe's possession. I feel that I deserve some small recompense for my information.'

A tremor ran through Roscoe, the sort of tremor that precedes a major earthquake.

'Small? SMALL? A hundred thousand dollars!'

'The customary agent's fee of ten per cent, sir.'

'You—'

'Please, sir!'

'Please, Roscoe!' said Mortimer Bayliss. 'Yes, I call that reasonable. If I'd been you, I'd have held out for halves. You do see, Roscoe, that he's got you in a cleft stick? Unless financially assisted, this other fellow won't get married for years and years, if ever. Who knows that he may not suddenly get a gleam of sense and realize that the only life is that of the bachelor? And you can't assist him financially if Keggs doesn't tell you who he is. You have your cheque-book, I know, because you never move without it. Give him his five thousand.'

'And have him tell me the wrong name again?' Roscoe laughed a mirthless laugh. 'I see myself!'

Mortimer Bayliss nodded.

'One appreciates the difficulty. You get it, Keggs? If you tell him the name before you have the cheque, he'll doublecross you and give you nothing, and until you tell him, he won't part. It begins to look like an impasse.'

'If I might be permitted to suggest a way out of the difficulty, sir. The name is one familiar to you, and you will recognize its authenticity. If I were to whisper it to you in confidence—'

'Excellent idea. Solves everything. Go ahead, Keggs. Whisper and I shall hear. . . . *Really!*' said Mortimer Bayliss with an exaggerated show of interest, as he took out a cambric handkerchief and dried his ear. 'Well, well, well! It's all right, Roscoe, this is the goods.'

While Roscoe sat plunged in gloomy thought, this way and that dividing the swift mind, like Sir Bedivere, Keggs went to the writing desk and took from one of its pigeonholes a sheet of paper. Placing it on a salver, for old butlerian habits were still strong, he presented it to Mortimer Bayliss.

'Hoping that Mr Bunyan might think well of my proposition, sir, I prepared a form of agreement, which only needs his signature to become legal. If you would care to glance at it?'

Mortimer Bayliss took the document, and screwed the monocle more firmly into his eye.

'You will see that it sets out quite clearly the circumstances and conditions, Mr Bayliss.'

'Very clearly. Is this a professional job?'

'No, sir, I did it myself with the assistance of *Every Man His Own Lawyer.*'

'Excellent bit of work. Come on, Roscoe. Out with the chequebook. But wait. I see the same objection we ran up against last time. How does he give Mr X. the money?'

'Very simply, sir. Mr Bunyan is the owner of the Bunyan Collection, of which you are curator. The young gentleman is in the Art business.'

'And so?'

'It would be perfectly understandable for Mr Bunyan to offer

him the post of assistant to yourself at a large salary, possibly
with the proviso that he would prefer to employ a married man
in that position. He might go so far as to hint that it would not
be long before the young gentleman succeeded to your place as
curator, you being old and past your work.'

'Here!'

'Merely a ruse, sir.'

'You may call it that. I call it blasphemy. Well, I get the idea,
but it seems tough on the poor fish. He'll give up his job and get
married, and then Roscoe will immediately fire him.'

'No, sir. Obviously there would have to be a definite written
agreement guaranteeing employment for a number of years.'

'One of those Every-Man-His-Own-Lawyer things of yours?'

'Precisely, sir. Otherwise the young gentleman would not have
the feeling of security necessary if he is to assume the responsi-
bilities of matrimony.'

'Or, in other words, feel safe in getting married?'

'Exactly, sir.'

'You think of everything, don't you?'

'I endeavour to do so, sir.'

Mortimer Bayliss waved a hand in the spacious gesture of the
man who is disposing of somebody else's money.

'Come on, Roscoe. Upsy-daisy. Sign here.'

'Eh?'

'Sign this paper, and you will hear who your rival is and all
about him, and then perhaps for God's sake I'll be able to go off
and get something to eat.'

A pleasant time was had by all at Barribault's excellent grill-room, Lord Uffenham, his spirits at their peak now that the dark menace of Stanhope Twine had been removed, being the life and soul of the party. From the opening slice of smoked salmon to the final demitasse he enchanted his audience, holding them spellbound with his tales of moving accidents by flood and field and hair-breadth 'scapes i' the imminent deadly breach in company with old Jacks and Joes and Jimmies of his distant youth. Though not all of them were 'scapes, for one of his best stories told how he and someone called Old Sammy on Boat Race night of the year 1911 had been taken by the insolent foe and on the following morning fined forty shillings at Bosher Street police station.

It was getting late when the Uffenham-Hollister-Benedick group of revellers drew up in Bill's car outside the front gate of Castlewood, and their arrival coincided with the breaking up of the business conference. As they alighted, Keggs, having deposited cheque and contract in the drawer of his writing-desk, was just escorting his visitors to the station wagon.

The well-nourished appearance of the Barribault trio gashed Mortimer Bayliss, who was now suffering the extreme of hunger, like a knife. It thrust on his mind thoughts of steaks and chops and juicy cuts off the joint, and in a rasping undertone he urged Roscoe, who was exchanging civilities with Lord Uffenham, for the love of Pete to cut it short and come along. But Roscoe had other views.

'Could I have a word with you, Hollister?' he said, and drew Bill aside.

Jane and Lord Uffenham went into the house, Mortimer Bayliss sat huddled in the station wagon, thinking of Hungarian goulash, and Roscoe spoke earnestly to Bill. And presently Lord Uffenham, curled up in his chair with his *Wonders of Bird Life*, saw his nephew-by-marriage-to-be enter, his face shining with a strange light.

'How right you were!' said Bill.

Lord Uffenham knew that he was always right about everything, but he was interested to learn to what particular exhibition of his rightness his young friend alluded.

'Which time was that?' he asked.

'When you said something would turn up. You saw Roscoe Bunyan buttonhole me just now?'

'Yerss, I saw him. Piefaced feller, that Bunyan.'

'I wish you wouldn't call him piefaced.'

'He *is* piefaced.'

'I know, but I wish you wouldn't say so, for you are speaking of the man I love.'

'He's a Tishbite.'

Bill was always reasonable.

'I admit he *looks* like a Tishbite,' he agreed, 'but beneath that Tishbitten exterior there is a sterling nature. He's just given me the most stupendous job.'

'Yer don't say?' Lord Uffenham was impressed. 'Must be good in the blighter, after all. I withdraw the word Tishbite.' He paused, reflecting. 'But not the word piefaced,' he added. 'Howjer mean a job? What sort of job?'

'One of the very finest. Let me take you step by step through our conversation. He started by asking me if I had ever thought of leaving the Gish Galleries.'

'To which yer replied?'

'That I had thought of it many a time and oft, but had always been deterred by the fear that, if I did, I might not be able to secure those three meals a day which are so essential to the man who wants to keep the roses in his cheeks. And then he tore off his whiskers and revealed himself as my guardian angel. Mortimer Bayliss, he said, is becoming senile and past his work, and how would I like to sign on as his assistant, eventually to take over the curatorship of the Bunyan Collection.'

'The what?'

'Roscoe's father, the late J. J. Bunyan, had one of the best collections of pictures in the world, and Roscoe inherited it. But let me tell you more. Having said this, he then named a salary – as a starter, mind you, just as a starter – which took my breath away. I'm rich!'

'Lord love a duck!'

'Rich enough, anyway, to support a wife who can do the cooking. I shall have to get busy, though. I've got to sail for America in a few days.'

'With Jane?'

'Well, of course with Jane. Good heavens, you don't think I'm going to leave her behind. How soon can one get married?'

'Like a flash, I believe, if yer get a special licence.'

'I'll get two, to be on the safe side.'

'I would. Can't go wrong, if yer have a spare.' Lord Uffenham was silent for a moment. He seemed deeply moved. 'Did yer know,' he said at length, 'that the Herring Gull, when it mates, swells its neck, opens its beak and regurgitates a large quantity of undigested food?'

'You don't say? That isn't a part of the Church of England marriage service, is it?'

'I believe not. Still,' said Lord Uffenham, 'it's an interesting thought. Makes yer realize that it takes all sorts to make a world.'

Roscoe Bunyan and Mortimer Bayliss, meanwhile, having driven off in the station wagon, had stopped it – at the latter's request – outside the Green Lion in Rosendale Road and had gone into that hostelry's saloon bar to eat cold ham. Mortimer Bayliss would have preferred *caviar frais, consommé aux pommes d'amour, suprême de foie gras au champagne, timbale de ris de veau Toulousiane* and *diablotins*, but, like Lord Uffenham, he could, when necessary, take the rough with the smooth. It would perhaps be too much to say that, when they resumed their journey to Shipley Hall, he was a ray of sunshine, but his mood had certainly changed for the better. He had leisure now to remember that Roscoe had just been separated from another five thousand pounds and had pledged himself legally to disburse a hundred thousand dollars, and this was a very stimulating thought. A little more of this, he was feeling, and the heir of the Bunyan millions would be growing so spiritual that his society would be a pleasure.

As they passed through the Shipley front door, Skidmore appeared.

'Excuse me, sir,' said Skidmore. 'Would you wish to speak to a Mr Pilbeam?'

'Pilbeam?' Roscoe started. 'Is he here?'

'No, sir. He rang up on the telephone while you were absent. He left his number.'

'Get through to him,' said Roscoe eagerly. 'I'll take the call in the smoking-room.'

'Very good, sir.'

'And bring me a cheese omelette and a pot of coffee and lots of toast and some of that fruit cake we had yesterday,' said Mortimer Bayliss.

He was in the morning-room, waiting for these necessaries, when Roscoe came in. His eye was bright, his manner animated.

'Pilbeam's got them,' he announced.

'Oh?' said Mortimer Bayliss, wrenching his thoughts away from the coming meal. 'Who is Pilbeam, and what has he got?'

'I told you about him. The fellow who runs the Argus Inquiry Agency. I hired him to get back those letters of mine.'

'Ah, yes. From your fiancée Eulalie Morningside or whatever her name is?'

'Elaine Dawn.'

'Is that her real name?'

'I suppose so.'

'I don't. I'll bet it's Martha Stubbs or something. So he's got them, has he? And now, I take it, you will notify the unfortunate girl that it's all off?'

'Of course.'

Mortimer Bayliss cackled.

'Love's young dream!' he said. 'We old bachelors will never understand it. You Romeos seem able to turn your affections on and off as if you were manipulating a tap. It's only a week ago that you were raving to me about her. You said she was wonderful. Why the devil don't you marry the girl?'

'And lose that million?'

'What do you want with another million? You don't need it.'

'Talk sense,' said Roscoe.

Mortimer Bayliss forbore to press the point. The door had opened, and the cheese omelette had arrived.

CHAPTER 19

The Argus Inquiry Agency, whose offices are in the south-western postal district of London, had come into being some years previously to fill a long-felt want . . . a want on the part of Percy Pilbeam, its founder, for more money. Starting out as editor of that celebrated weekly scandal sheet, *Society Spice*, he had wearied after a while of nosing out people's discreditable secrets for a salary, and had come to the conclusion that a man of his gifts would be doing far better for himself nosing out such secrets on his own behalf. Having borrowed some capital, he had handed in his portfolio, and was now in very good shape financially. It was the boast of the Argus that it never slept, and this, felt those who knew it, was, if it possessed a conscience, not surprising. Few would have been able to sleep with what the Argus Inquiry Agency had on its mind.

In engaging a private investigator, the prudent man sets more value on astuteness than on physical beauty, and in the case of the guiding spirit of the Argus this was fortunate, for though it was possible that there may have been more repellent human bloodhounds in London than Percy Pilbeam, they would have taken a considerable amount of finding. He was a small, weedy, heavily pimpled young man with eyes set too close together, whose flannel suit looked like a Neapolitan ice and whose upper lip was disfigured by a wispy and revolting moustache. The overall picture he presented as Roscoe entered his office on the following morning was one calculated to jar on the sensitive eye, but to Roscoe, so profound was his relief that the fatal papers had been recovered, that he looked quite attractive. He took the little packet of stationery with uplifted heart.

'Swell!' he said sunnily. 'How did you manage to get them?'

Percy Pilbeam ran a pen airily through his brilliantined hair.

'Easy. She has to be at the theatre every night. I waited till she had gone, got in, hunted around, found the letters and got out again. It was simple. Well, when I say simple,' said Pilbeam, belatedly thinking of the bill he would be sending in, 'it wasn't by any means. There was great risk involved. And of course the nervous strain.'

'Oh, you wouldn't mind that,' said Roscoe, also thinking of the bill. 'Not a man of your experience. You told me you were always doing that sort of thing.'

'Nevertheless . . . I beg your pardon?'

'You said something.'

This was inaccurate. Roscoe had not spoken, he had given a sudden gurgle, and he had gurgled suddenly because a thought had come like a full-blown rose, flushing his brow. It was not often that he received anything in the nature of an inspiration, for his brain moved as a rule rather sluggishly, but one had come to him now, and it had shaken him to the soles of his shoes.

Even the most stolid have their dreams, and ever since his visit to Castlewood visions had been rising before Roscoe's eyes of somehow getting that contract away from Keggs and tearing it up, thus drawing the subtle butler's fangs and rendering him no longer a force for evil. And he had thought of a capital way of doing this, a plan complete in every detail. The only objection to it was that to carry it out called for nerve, and his own nerve was insufficient. He needed an ally, and it had suddenly occurred to him that in Pilbeam he had found one.

'Look,' he said. 'I want you to take on another job for me.'

'What kind?'

'The same kind.'

'You mean you've written some *more* letters?'

There was surprise in Pilbeam's voice, and also something not very far from an awed admiration. This would make the third lot of compromising letters penned by this client, a so far undisputed record. Even baronets, so notoriously lax in their moral outlook, had been content with two.

Roscoe hastened to dispel the idea that he had been setting up a mark for all other takers of pen in hand to shoot at.

'No, no, it isn't letters this time. It's a paper, a document.'

'The Naval Treaty?' said Pilbeam, who had his lighter moments.

'It's a sort of agreement.'

Pilbeam began to understand.

'I see. Something you signed?'

'Yes.'

'And you want to get out of it?'

'That's it. And the only way to get out of it is to—'

'Pinch it? Quite. Yes, I see that. And if I follow you correctly, you are suggesting that I do it?'

'Yes.'

'H'm.'

'It would be perfectly easy,' said Roscoe persuasively. 'The man who's got it is a fellow named Keggs. He used to be my father's butler years ago, and he's retired now and lives in Valley Fields. He owns some house property down there. All you would have to do is call on him and say you come from me and you're looking for a house and has he anything that would suit you. He'll probably be tickled to death, because I happen to know that the man who had one of his houses has just come into a lot of money and is sure to be leaving. Well, that gets you into the place, and when he brings out the drinks – he's bound to bring out drinks – you slip a kayo drop into his, and there you are. Simple as falling off a log,' said Roscoe encouragingly. He looked at the other in rather a pained way. 'Why,' he asked, 'do you say "H'm"?'

It took Pilbeam but an instant to explain why he had said 'H'm'.

'I was wondering why, if it's as simple as all that, you don't do it yourself,' he said nastily.

Roscoe hesitated. The question had put him in something of a difficulty. His actual reason for not wishing to revisit Castle-wood was one he preferred to keep from the man whom he was hoping to send there as his representative. At one point in the business conference which had culminated in the signing of the contract, a bulldog of ruffianly aspect had looked in at the door, coughed in a menacing way and gone out. It had seemed to Roscoe, who was timid with dogs, that the animal, just before withdrawing, had given him a look as menacing as its cough, and nothing would have induced him to risk encountering it again. (Actually, George had coughed to attract the attention of the occupants of the room in case any of them had cake to dispose of – had been told by his sixth sense that there was no hope of cake – and had gone off to try to find Jane, who was usually good for a hand-out. The menace of his parting look had existed purely in Roscoe's imagination.)

'He would be on his guard against me,' he said, inspired. 'I'd never get to first base. But he wouldn't dream there was anything wrong about you.'

This was plausible, and Pilbeam recognized it as such. Nevertheless he shook his head. The scheme as outlined by Roscoe did not offend his moral sense, for he had not got one, but it struck him as too hazardous for comfort. At a never to be forgotten point in his search of Miss Dawn's apartment the doorbell had suddenly rung, and he had distinctly felt his heart leap from its base and crash into his front teeth. He shrank from a repetition of that experience.

He mentioned this to Roscoe. Roscoe pooh-poohed his qualms.

'But, good Lord, man, this wouldn't be like that. You wouldn't be breaking in. You'd just be paying an ordinary call.'

Pilbeam continued to shake his head.

'Sorry...' he was beginning, when Roscoe went on.

'I'd be prepared to pay something special.'

Pilbeam's head ceased to shake. He wavered. Just as Roscoe liked making another million, so did he enjoy being paid something special.

'What is this agreement you speak of?' he asked, interested but refraining from committing himself.

'Oh, just an agreement,' said Roscoe. His native prudence forbade him to tell all. The private investigator who learns that he is saving a client a hundred thousand dollars is a private investigator who puts his prices up.

'What does it look like?'

'It's just a paper. He put it in an envelope and wrote something on the outside – "Agreement" or "Contract" or "In re R. Bunyan, Esquire", I suppose, or something like that. And then he locked it away in a drawer of the writing table.'

Pilbeam reflected. His sales resistance was weakening.

'So it would not mean a long search?'

'You would lay your hands on it in half a minute. Just break open the drawer. Nothing else to it.'

'If I were caught breaking open a drawer in someone else's house, I'd be sent to prison.'

'Rather pleasant places, prisons, these days, they tell me.'

'*Who* tells you?'

'Oh, one hears it around. Movies, concerts, entertainments, all that sort of thing. Besides, who would catch you?'

'Who else is in the house?'

'Lord Uffenham and his niece.'

'There you are, then.'

Roscoe refused to admit that there he was.

'Perfectly easy to get rid of them. Make it Saturday, and I'll send the old boy a couple of tickets for a matinée. That'll fix it. Nobody ever refuses free theatre tickets.'

Pilbeam fondled his distressing little moustache for a moment. Then he asked the question Roscoe had been hoping he would not ask.

'How about dogs?'

Roscoe hesitated. Then he saw that there was nothing for it but to come clean. All might well be lost, were this private investigator to find himself, unprepared, confronted with that bulldog. He judged others by himself, and he himself, if he had been rifling a drawer in a strange house and a bulldog had happened along, would have dropped everything and run like the wind. Concealment was useless. Now it must be told.

'There is a dog,' he admitted.

'What sort of a dog?'

'A bulldog.'

'H'm.'

'Very friendly animals, bulldogs, I believe.'

'If you believe that, you'll believe anything. I knew a man who got mixed up with a bulldog, and he had to have seven stitches.'

Inspiration came to Roscoe for the second time that morning.

'I'll tell you what I'll do,' he said. 'If you will go and attend to this man Keggs on Saturday afternoon, I'll go there on Friday night and give the dog a chunk of doctored meat.'

Pilbeam frowned. Stoutly though those who knew him would have denied it, he had certain scruples. He did not look human, but he was not without human feelings.

'I don't like poisoning dogs.'

'Oh, I wouldn't *poison* him. Just give him something that would make him take to his bed next day. Any vet will tell me the right dose.'

'How would you contact this dog?'

'No difficulty about that. He's sure to be out in the garden this fine weather. I know the man who lives next door. I'll go and see him and drop the stuff over the fence.' He paused, eyeing his companion pleadingly. 'So you will do it, won't you?'

Pilbeam sat plunged in thought. Almost Roscoe had persuaded him. He liked this dog sequence. Unquestionably it would make his path straight. And he knew Roscoe to be a man of many millions, well able to pay for his whims.

'I'll do it for a thousand pounds, cash down,' he said, and a sharp pang shot through Roscoe, not unlike a twinge of sciatica.

'A thousand pounds?'

'Didn't I speak distinctly?' said Pilbeam coldly. His sensitive soul resented anything in the nature of haggling.

Once more, as had happened at the business conference, Roscoe found himself in the unpleasant position of sipping the bitter cup. He had no choice but to agree, but mentally he was totting up the roster of the sprats which he was being compelled to distribute in order to catch the whale, and their number and bulk appalled him.

'You wouldn't feel like doing it for a hundred, would you?' he asked wistfully.

Pilbeam said he would not.

'A thousand pounds is a lot of money.'

'Quite,' said Pilbeam, jauntily massaging the third pimple from the left on his right cheek. 'That's why I like it.'

In stating that no one ever refused free seats for the theatre, Roscoe Bunyan had shown a firm grasp of human psychology. The matinée tickets, arriving at Castlewood by the first post on Friday, were received with the utmost enthusiasm. Lord Uffenham though abating no whit of his opinion that their donor was piefaced, commended him heartily for his kindly thought, saying that it was dashed civil of the young blighter, and even Jane had to admit that in the years that had passed since their mixed bathing days at Meadowhampton Roscoe must have improved out of all knowledge. Joy, in short, on the Friday might have been said to have reigned supreme.

But on Saturday morning the sun went behind the clouds, for tragedy hit the home. Lord Uffenham, going to George the bulldog's basket to rout him out for his pre-breakfast airing, found him inert, his nose warm, his manner listless, his stump of a tail with not so much as a quiver in it. The dullest eye could perceive that the dumb chum was seriously below par, and Lord Uffenham lost no time in summoning his colleagues for a consultation.

'Jay-un!'

'Hullo?'

'Keggs!'

'M'lord?'

'Cummere. Something wrong with George.'

Gravely the three gathered at the sick-bed. Lips were pursed, heads shaken. 'Oh, George, my precious angel!' cried Jane, and 'Most extraordinary' said Keggs, as indeed it was, for until now the invalid's health had always been of the robustest. His reputation was that of a dog able to eat tenpenny nails and thrive on them.

Approving their concern but feeling that it did not go far enough, Lord Uffenham struck the practical note, and became executive.

'Keggs!'

'M'lord?'

'Where's the nearest vet?'

'Offhand I could not say, m'lord, but I could ascertain by consulting the classified telephone directory.'

'Go and do it, my dear feller.'

'And make it snappy,' said Jane. 'Of course,' she went on, as Keggs departed on his errand of mercy, 'this dishes our theatre party.'

'Hey? Why?'

'Well, we can't go off and leave poor George on a bed of pain. We'll have to scratch the binge.'

'Nonsense. Can't waste theatre tickets. You go, I'll stay with George. Go and give Fred Holloway a buzz—'

'Hollister.'

'Holloway or Hollister, the point is immaterial. Get him on the 'phone and tell him to take you to this bally theatre.'

'But it seems so selfish.'

'Hey?'

'Leaving you here. You were looking forward to your little treat.'

'Not a bit of it. Just as soon stay at home with my book.'

'Couldn't Mr Keggs look after George?'

'Wouldn't be equal to it. George needs a father's care. He will have to be chirruped to, and I doubt if Keggs is any good at chirruping. You do as I tell you.'

'Well, all right, if you say so.'

'You'll enjoy an afternoon out with your young man.'

'I shall,' said Jane, with conviction.

The morning passed. The veterinary surgeon called, diagnosed George's complaint as stomachic, giving it as his opinion that he must have picked up something poisonous, and went away assuring them that rest and a light diet and the mixture every three hours would in time effect a cure. Bill arrived in his car and took Jane off to lunch and the theatre. And Lord Uffenham and George settled down for the afternoon, the former in his chair with *Wonders Of The Bird World*, the latter in his basket with a woolly rug over him. And all was quiet on the Castlewood front till about half-past four, when a young man in a Neapolitan ice suit and blue suede shoes turned in at the front gate and rang the door-bell. It was Percy Pilbeam, up and coming.

Right-minded people cannot, of course, but look askance at Percy Pilbeam, for his was a code of ethics that left much to be desired, and yet those of tender heart must surely, we think, find that heart bleeding a little for the unfortunate private investigator as he walks so gaily into this house of peril, supposing it to be unoccupied except for Augustus Keggs. As he stands there, waiting for the bell to be answered and stroking his regrettable moustache, no thought is in his mind of a fifteen stone Viscount lurking on the premises.

Had all gone according to plan, there should have been a complete absence of fifteen stone Viscounts, but, as we have seen, all had not gone according to plan. It just proves, if proof were needed, that the best-laid plans of mice and men gang oft agley. The poet Burns, it will be remembered, has commented on this.

The door opened.

'Mr Keggs?' said Pilbeam.

'Yes, sir.'

'Good afternoon. I was sent by Mr Bunyan, who tells me he is an old friend of yours. I am looking for a house down here, and he thought you might have one that would suit me.'

'Yes, indeed, sir,' said Keggs, who had learned that morning from Stanhope Twine that Peacehaven would no longer be required by him. 'If you will step this way.'

'Charming spot, Valley Fields,' said Percy Pilbeam. 'I ought to have come here years ago.'

'The loss is ours, sir,' said Augustus Keggs courteously.

For Lord Uffenham the afternoon had passed not unpleasantly. He had finished *Wonders of Bird Life*, done quite a bit of chirruping to George, smoked a mild cigar and dozed off for half an hour or so. At five o'clock, George having fallen into a refreshing sleep and seeming able now to carry on under his own steam without a father to watch over him, he wandered out into the garden for a breath of air.

Among the first things that met his eye in the garden was a handsome snail, and he stood staring at it with unblinking gaze, his always inquiring mind concentrated on the problem of how snails, handicapped as they are by having no legs, manage nevertheless to get from point to point at so creditable a rate of speed. The one under advisement, though not a Roger Bannister, was unmistakably on its way somewhere and going all out, and he sought in vain for an explanation of this nippiness. He was still brooding on the mystery, when Mortimer Bayliss appeared.

Mortimer Bayliss, though inclined to be brusque with his fellow men, was not without his softer side, and he had taken a great liking to Lord Uffenham, who reminded him of an elephant on which, when a boy, he had often ridden at the Bronx Zoo. He wished him well and was sorry that he had had to tell him the bad news about those pictures. A nasty knock it must have been, he felt, for the poor old buster to learn that what he had in his gallery and had hoped to raise money on was not the work of Gainsborough and Constable but of Wilfred Robinson and Sidney Biffen. When, therefore, a more detailed inspection revealed some quite decent stuff that had unaccountably been overlooked by the previous five Viscounts, it was with something of the feeling of a Boy Scout about to do his day's act of kindness that he had climbed into Roscoe's Jaguar, now happily recovered from its ailments, and driven to Castlewood to bring him the welcome tidings.

'Oh, there you are,' he said, coming into the garden. 'I've been ringing the bell, but nothing happened. Is everybody dead in this lazar house?'

'Hey?' said Lord Uffenham, emerging from his trance. 'Oh, hullo, Banstead. Ringing, did yer say? Odd Keggs didn't hear yer. Asleep, I suppose. He takes a nap in the afternoon. I've been watching a snail.'

'Always watch snails,' said Mortimer Bayliss approvingly. 'It is the secret of a happy and successful life. A snail a day keeps the doctor away.'

'You ever pondered on snails?'

'Only intermittently, if at all.'

'I was wondering how they get around, the way they do. Look

at this one. Breezing along like a two-year-old with its chin up and its chest out. How does it do it without any legs?'

'Will power, I should imagine. You can't keep a good snail down. Well, you're probably wondering why I'm here, though no doubt delighted to see me. I came to tell you that things aren't as bad as I gave you to understand when I saw you at Shipley that day. Those pictures. Some of them, I find, are all right.'

'Worth money?'

'Quite a good bit.'

'Well, that's capital. That's excellent. Things are certainly looking up. My luck's in. Ever noticed how everything seems to go right, when yer luck's in? You met my niece the other night, didn't yer—?'

'For a moment. Charming girl.'

'Yerss, not so dusty. Well, until that night she was all tied up with about the worst piece of cheese in Valley Fields. But no longer. She's seen the light and is now engaged to that splendid feller Holloway.'

'Hollister.'

'Everybody keeps saying Hollister. Suppose I've got the name wrong. I sometimes do. I remember now he's a friend of yours.'

'I've known him all his life.'

'Fine young chap.'

'One of the best. I curse him for the good of his soul, but I love him like an uncle. Pity he's so hard up.'

'But he isn't. That's what I was going to tell yer. That feller Bunyan's given him an excellent job.'

'He has? Well, well, well! Very altruistic young man, Roscoe Bunyan. Always doing these kindnesses.' A cackle escaped Mortimer Bayliss. 'So he's given him a job, has he?'

'Yerss. Something to do with some picture collection he owns.'

'Assistant to the curator?'

'That's right, and guaranteed him the curator job as soon as he can get rid of the present chap. The present chap's no good.'

'No good, eh?'

'No. Gone all senile, I gather. Ah well, none of us get younger.'

'Thank goodness.'

'Hey?'

'What hell it would be, if we did. Think of the risks you run of getting married, when you're young.'

'That's true,' said Lord Uffenham, who all through his early twenties had been in constant peril.

'No young man is safe. By the mercy of Providence I managed to stay single in my hot youth, but it was a near thing once or twice, and I wouldn't care to have to go through it again. How well I remember that awful, haunting fear that at any moment some unguarded word would land me in the Niagara Falls hotel with rice dropping off me. I am speaking, of course, of the days when I still had hair and teeth and was known as Beau Bayliss, the days when a flick of my finger meant a broken heart. Yes, I got through, but few are as lucky as I was. If I had my way, marriage would be forbidden by law.'

'Wouldn't the human race die out?'

'Yes, and what a break that would be for everybody. Think of a world without any Bunyans in it.'

'Yer don't like Roscoe Bunyan?'

'I do not.'

'Nor me. Bit of a gumboil, I should describe him as. He was down here yesterday evening. I saw him in the garden next door. He was chatting with George over the fence.'

'Who's George?'

'My bulldog. He's not well today.'

'Who would be after chatting with Roscoe Bunyan? I've had two weeks of him, and it has aged me a dozen years. It must sadden you to think of a fellow like that at Shipley.'

'Yerss. Unpleasant, losing yer old home. Not that I'm not comfortable here.'

'Odd that you should be living cheek by jowl with my friend Keggs.'

'Not so particularly odd. He used to be my butler.'

'Oh, I see. That would, of course, bring you very close together. How do you split up the house?'

'He has the ground floor, and Jane and I the upstairs. It's like two separate flats. Works very well. Come and have a look at his quarters. He'll be glad to show yer round. He's very proud of the way he's fixed himself up, and I don't blame him. He's as snug as a bug in a rug.'

They went round the angle of the house. Mortimer Bayliss paused to pick a flower. Lord Uffenham, reaching the french windows, halted abruptly, stared, his lips moving in a silent 'Lord love a duck!', and came tiptoeing back to his companion, who was putting the flower in his buttonhole.

'Hey!' he whispered.

'Got laryngitis?' asked Mortimer Bayliss.

'No, no laryngitis.'

'Then why are you talking like a leaky cistern?'

Lord Uffenham put a warning finger to his lips.

'I'll tell yer why I'm talking like a leaky cistern,' he said, still speaking in that conspiratorial whisper. 'There's a bally burglar in there!'

Very few things were able to disconcert Mortimer Bayliss. The monocle in his eye did not even quiver.

'A burglar, eh?' he said, as if he had ordered one from the stores and was glad to learn that it had arrived safely.

'That's right. Keggs is lying on the floor, out like a light, and there's a horrible bounder at the desk, going through his effects. I didn't know burglars ever burgled in the daytime,' said Lord Uffenham with the disapproval which men of orthodox outlook always show when their attention is drawn to any deviation from the normal. 'Always had the idea they only came out after dark.'

'You're thinking of dramatic critics. What sort of a burglar is it?'

Lord Uffenham found himself puzzled, as any man might be when called on to supply a word-portrait of a marauder.

'How d'yer mean, what sort?'

'Big? The large economy size?'

'No, small.'

'Then come on,' said Mortimer Bayliss with enthusiasm. There was a spade beside the flower bed in which on the previous evening, wishing to discipline his figure, Lord Uffenham had been doing a little digging. 'What are we waiting for? Let's go!'

* * *

And so it came about that Percy Pilbeam, in the act of thrusting into his pocket a manilla envelope inscribed with the words 'In re R. Bunyan, Esq.', experienced once more that unpleasant sensation of having his heart leap into his mouth and loosen a front tooth. He had supposed himself to be alone – except for Keggs, who hardly counted – and lo, of a sudden a voice, sounding to his sensitive ear like that of Conscience, shattered the afternoon stillness with a stentorian 'Hey!'. Just the sort of thing the voice of Conscience might have been expected to say.

He whirled on his axis, hastily gulping his heart down again. There, looming massively inside the french windows, stood the largest man he had ever seen and, accompanying him, a friend and well-wisher holding a substantial spade. The day was warm, but cold shivers ran down his spine. He felt, gazing upon these twain, that their attitude foreboded violence, and violence was a thing which, for he was not one of your tough Marlows or Mike Hammers, he feared and disliked. In the hope of easing a difficult situation, he smiled what was intended to be an ingratiating smile, and said 'Oh, hullo'.

It had the worst effect.

'Hullo to you, with knobs on,' retorted Lord Uffenham curtly. He turned to Mortimer Bayliss as to one on whose sympathy he could rely. 'He grins', he said, a querulous note in his voice. 'We catch him burgling the house, catch him redhanded, as the expression is, and he *grins*. He says "Oh, hullo", and GRINS. Like a ruddy Cheshire cat. Have that spade ready, Banstead.'

Percy Pilbeam, as if about to have his photograph taken, moistened his lips with the tip of his tongue. His brow was wet with dishonest sweat.

'I'm not burgling,' he bleated weakly.

Lord Uffenham clicked his tongue. He did not mind hearing people talk poppycock, but it must not be utter poppycock.

'Don't be silly. If yer don't call it burgling to sneak into a feller's sitting-room and lay him out cold with a blunt instrument and loot his bally desk, there are finer-minded men who do. Stick tightly to the spade, Banstead, we may be needing it at any moment.'

Mortimer Bayliss was bending over the form on the floor, examining it with an experienced eye. In what he had called his hot youth he had often seen fellow-customers in saloons lying on floors like that, and he knew the procedure.

'Not a blunt instrument,' he said. 'The impression I get is that my old friend has been slipped a knock-out drop.'

'Hey?'

'I don't believe you see much of them in England, but in America, notably in New York down Eighth and Ninth Avenue way, and particularly on Saturday nights, you might say they are common form. Did you slip him a knock-out drop, blot?'

'Answer the question,' thundered Lord Uffenham, as the blot hesitated coyly. 'Yes or no?'

'Er – yes.'

Lord Uffenham snorted.

'You see! A full confession. What shall we do with him? Break him into little bits? Or shall I beetle round to the police station and gather in a constable or two?'

Mortimer Bayliss was silent for a space, weighing the question. Then he spoke, and his words were music to Percy Pilbeam's ears.

'I think we might let him go.'

Lord Uffenham started. He stared incredulously. His bulging eye was like that of a tiger to whom the suggestion has been made that it shall part with its breakfast coolie.

'Let him *go*?'

'After a few simple preliminaries. I remember reading a story once,' said Mortimer Bayliss, adjusting his monocle, 'that has always stuck in my mind. It was about a burglar who burgled a house and the owner caught him and held him up with a gun and made him take all his clothes off and then showed him politely out of the front door. It struck me as an excellent idea.'

'A most admirable idea,' assented Lord Uffenham warmly. He was remorseful that for an instant he had wronged this splendid fellow in thought. 'Nothing could be more suitable.'

'Good for a laugh, I think?'

'Dashed amusing. Very droll. What was it you called this bounder just now?'

'A blot?'

'That's right. Off with your clothes, blot.'

Percy Pilbeam quivered like an aspen. There rose before him the picture of Roscoe Bunyan assuring him that he would find this house unoccupied, and a wave of anti-Roscoe sentiment flooded over him. Few men with pimples have ever felt more bitter toward a man with a double chin.

'But—' he began.

'Did I hear you say "But"?' said Lord Uffenham.

'Yes, don't say "But",' said Mortimer Bayliss. 'We want willing service and selfless co-operation. The trousers first, I think.'

Lord Uffenham was musing, a finger to his cheek.

'Here's a thought, Banstead. Why not paint him black?'

'Have you black paint?'

'Plenty.'

'It would look very pretty,' said Mortimer Bayliss thoughtfully. 'Yes, I can see him with a coat of black paint.'

'Could I have a drink?' said Percy Pilbeam.

He spoke pleadingly, and Lord Uffenham, though in stern mood, saw no reason why justice should not be tempered with mercy to this small extent. He waved hospitably at the table where the syphon and decanter stood, and Pilbeam tottered to it and poured himself a brimming beaker.

'Or green?' said Lord Uffenham, and was about to inform his friend that he possessed green paint as well as black and to ask him if he did not think Pilbeam would look better in green – snappier, dressier, better in every way – but at this moment his remarks were interrupted by the receipt between the eyes of two-thirds of a long whisky-and-soda. It gave him the passing sensation of having been caught in an explosion at a distillery.

In delineating Percy Pilbeam, we have stressed that he was neither brave nor beautiful, but we have shown him also, we fancy, as a young man with plenty of brains and one capable of thinking quickly in an emergency. He had thought quickly now. To fling his beverage in Lord Uffenham's face and dart to the french windows had been with him the work of an inspired instant. A whirring noise, and he was out in the open and going like the wind.

Riper years and a chronic stiffness in the joints prevented Lord Uffenham and Mortimer Bayliss answering his challenge with a similar burst of speed. They, too, passed into the open, but their progress, when there, could not have been compared to even the gentlest breeze. They moved slowly and jerkily, like rheumatic buffaloes, and it is not surprising that, on arrival at the front gate, they should have found a total shortage of private investigators. Pilbeam had gone, leaving not a wrack behind. All they saw was Bill and Jane standing by Bill's car, gazing interestedly down the road.

'Who,' Bill asked, becoming aware of their presence, 'was the jack rabbit?'

'Something in a striped suit came whizzing past us,' said Jane.

'Wearing pimples with a red tie,' said Bill. 'A mistake, I think. One or the other, but not both.'

Jane gave a sudden squeak of concern.

'Uncle George! You're wet.'

'I know I'm wet,' said Lord Uffenham morosely. 'Who wouldn't be, with burglars drenching them with whisky-and-sodas all the time? I'm going in to change. Might catch a nasty cold.'

He went moodily into the house, and Jane turned to Mortimer Bayliss.

'Burglars?' she said. 'Was there a burglar?'

'There was, indeed, I took up this spade to quell him. Now that he is no longer here to be quelled, I'll be putting it back,' said Mr Bayliss, and went off to do so.

'Burglars!' said Jane. 'Just imagine.'

'Valley Fields for excitement.'

'You ought to be saying "There, there, little woman" and putting your arms about me and telling me to fear nothing, for you are here.'

'A very admirable suggestion,' said Bill.

Behind them somebody coughed. Keggs was standing there, his face contorted with pain. He had a severe headache, and even that soft cough had accentuated it.

'Oh, hullo, Mr Keggs,' said Bill. 'We were – er – just discussing the wedding arrangements.'

'I should not advocate an immediate wedding, sir,' said Keggs sepulchrally.

In the mind of Augustus Keggs when, waking like Abou ben Adhem from a deep dream of peace, he found that he had acquired the headache of a lifetime and lost the manilla envelope inscribed 'In re R. Bunyan Esq.', there had been at first not unnaturally a certain disorder, but from the welter of confused emotions two coherent thoughts stood out. One was the intention to go to the chemist's in Rosendale Road, if he could navigate so far, and get the most powerful pick-me-up the man behind the counter could provide; the other a stern resolve to be revenged upon Roscoe Bunyan for the outrage he had perpetrated, an outrage so dastardly that few international gangs, however tough, would have cared to include it in their programmes.

For that the hidden hand behind both headache and robbery had been that of Roscoe he did not for an instant doubt. When a man with a moustache and pimples calls on a retired butler saying that he has been sent by Mr Bunyan, and proceeds to doctor the retired butler's drink and purloin the contract whereby Mr Bunyan has pledged himself to pay the retired butler a hundred thousand dollars, the retired butler, unless very slow at the uptake, is able to deduce and form his own conclusions. He sees in what direction the evidence points and in compiling his list of suspects knows where to look.

So now, with a view to foiling Roscoe's plans and aims, Keggs, though he would have preferred to go straight to Rosendale Road for that pick-me-up, halted on seeing Bill, and said:

'I should not advocate an immediate wedding, sir.'

And while Bill stared at him, his eyes narrowing as our eyes are so apt to do when we are confronted with a speaker whom we suspect of having had a couple, he added:

'If I might have your attention for a moment, Mr Hollister.'

Both Shakespeare (William) and Pope (Alexander) have stressed the tediousness of a twice-told tale, and a thrice-told tale is, of course, even worse. At two points already in this chronicle the story of Mortimer Bayliss's matrimonial tontine has been placed before the reader, and anyone so intelligent must, one feels, by this time have got the idea. No need, accordingly, to report Keggs's words verbatim. Sufficient to say that on this occasion, though hampered by shooting pains that started at the soles of his feet and got worse all the way up, he placed the facts before Bill and Jane as lucidly as some days earlier he had placed them before Roscoe Bunyan. And he found an audience equally receptive. Bill, as the narrative proceeded, stared at him dumbly. So did Jane. Then, as he concluded his remarks, they stared at one another dumbly.

'You mean,' said Bill, transferring his pop-eyed gaze to Keggs, 'that if I get married, I lose a million dollars?'

'If at the time of your embarkation on matrimony Mr Roscoe is still single, yes, sir.'

'And he's not even engaged, as far as I know.'

'No, sir.'

It was some days since Bill had drawn one of those deep breaths of his, but he drew one now. A man to whom the skulduggery of a Roscoe Bunyan has been suddenly revealed in all its naked horror is entitled to draw a deep breath or two.

'So that was why he gave me that job! To put me out of the running.'

'Exactly, sir. It was a ruse or scheme.'

'The hound!'

'Yes, sir.'

'The heel!'

'Yes, sir.'

'The slimy, slithering serpent!'

'Precisely, sir,' said Keggs, in cordial agreement with the view that Roscoe Bunyan shared the low cunning and general lack of charm of the reptile he had mentioned. 'Mr Roscoe sticks at nothing, as one might say. Even as a growing lad, so I am informed by friends who remained in the service of the late Mr Bunyan, his behaviour was characterized by the same lack of scruple. At the age of fifteen he was expelled from his school for lending money to his fellow students at ruinous rates of interest. The child,' said Keggs, 'is the father of the man.'

'The child should have been drowned in a bucket at birth,' said Bill severely. 'Then he wouldn't have become a man. But will anyone adopt these simple home remedies nowadays? Oh, no. Old-fashioned, they say, and what's the result? Roscoe Bunyan. Eh?'

'I merely said "Ouch!" sir. I have a somewhat severe headache. I was about to go to the chemist's in the hope of procuring some specific that might alleviate it.'

'Oh? Then we mustn't keep you. I know what it is to have a headache. This bombshell of yours has given me one. Off you go.'

'Thank you very much, sir,' said Keggs, and with a hand pressed to his throbbing brow passed painfully on his way, headed for Rosendale Road and its pick-me-ups.

He left behind him a stunned silence. It was Bill who finally broke it.

'Well, that's that,' he said. 'Too bad. I'd have liked a million dollars.'

Jane looked at him, wide-eyed.

'Bill! What do you mean?'

'Well, wouldn't anyone?'

'You aren't going ahead with the wedding now?'

'Of course I am. I've got to take this job of Roscoe's. I turned in my resignation to Gish the day before yesterday. I have to sail for America on Wednesday.'

'But you don't have to get married first.'

Bill stared.

'Are you suggesting that I leave you behind?'

'It would only mean waiting a little.'

'A *little*?' Bill barked derisively. 'You don't know R. Bunyan. Now he's on to it that he'll lose a million dollars if he gets married, he won't get married till he's seventy, if then. Pretty silly we should look, going on year after year, you here, me in America, exchanging picture postcards and waiting hopefully for Roscoe to walk down the aisle with a gardenia in his buttonhole.'

'But think of the plans we made, all the things we were going to do if we ever had money. Don't you remember, that day at Barribault's? You were going to take up your painting again, and I was going to get Shipley back for Uncle George.'

'I know, I know. Well, I'll have to do without my painting, and Uncle George will have to do without Shipley. Good heavens, young fathead, what do you think would happen to me, if I went off to America and left you here? I'd go steadily crazy. I'd be thinking all the time of all the sons of bachelors who were flocking round you, trying to get you away from me.'

'You know I'd never look at another man.'

'Why not? I'm nothing special. Just one of the swineherds, and not the best of them by any manner of means.'

'One of the *what*?'

'In the fairy stories you read as a child. Surely you used to read fairy stories where the princess fell in love with the swineherd? The point I am making is that there you would be, surrounded by princes, all doing their damnedest to de-swineherd you, and after a time you'd be bound to wonder if it was worth while going on waiting for William Hollister.'

'You are speaking of William *Quackenbush* Hollister?'

'The same.'

'Well, I wouldn't wonder anything of the sort. I'd wait for you through all eternity, Bill, you old ass, and you know it.'

'Yes, you think that now, but would you feel the same at the end of the first five years, with Roscoe still sitting tight and cannily refusing offers of marriage on all sides? I see you weakening. I see you saying to yourself "Who is this bird Hollister, anyway? Where does he get off, expecting to—"'

'"— take the best years of my life"?'

'Exactly. No, sir! You'll come with me on Wednesday, like a good girl, and to hell with all tontines.'

Janes eyes were glowing.

'Oh, Bill! Am I really worth a million dollars to you?'

'More. Considerably more. Any man who gets a girl like you for a mere million bucks has driven a shrewd bargain.'

'Oh, *Bill*!' said Jane, and Keggs, returning some minutes later from his travels, found himself compelled to cough once more.

CHAPTER 23

But this time the cough brought no attendant anguish with it. It is pleasant to be able to record that Augustus Keggs's confidence in the man behind the counter at the Rosendale Road chemist's had not been misplaced. The fellow knew his pick-me-ups. He was good. He had taken a little of this from one bottle, a little of that from another bottle, added dynamite and red pepper and handed the mixture to his suffering client, and it was not long before the latter, reassured that a hydrogen bomb had not, as at the outset of the proceedings he had feared, been exploded in his interior, was able to return to his cosy living-room almost as good as new.

He found Lord Uffenham there. In flannel trousers and a sweater which might have been built to order by Omar the Tent-Maker, the now dry Viscount was brooding ponderously over the bowl of goldfish.

'Ants' eggs,' he said, as Keggs entered. 'Why ants' eggs? Hey?'

'M'lord?'

'I've been wondering how the dickens goldfish acquired a taste for ants' eggs.'

'They like them, m'lord.'

'I know they like them. What I'm saying is how did they come to like them? In their natural, wild state I don't see how they could ever have established contact with ants. Lord love a duck, man, you don't suppose the ancestors of these goldfish used to come ashore and roam the countryside hoping to find an ant-hill where they could help themselves to a dish of eggs, do you? Oh, well, there it is,' said Lord Uffenham philosophically, and turned to another aspect of life among the ants. 'Did yer know they run quicker in warm weather?'

'M'lord?'

'Ants. When the weather's warm, they run quicker.'

'Indeed, m'lord?'

'So I read somewhere. In the summer months they clip quite a bit off their winter time and dash all over the place like billy-o. Which reminds me. There was someone on the 'phone for you just now. A Mrs Billson. Name convey anything to you?'

'My sister, m'lord.'

'Oh, your sister? I was forgetting yer had a sister. I had three at one time,' said Lord Uffenham with modest pride. 'Well, she wants you to call her.'

During the rather lengthy period of Keggs's telephoning Lord Uffenham continued to brood, first over the goldfish and then over the canary in its cage. The canary was eating groundsel, a thing his lordship would not have done on a bet, and, absorbed in his meditations on the bird's peculiar tastes, he heard nothing of what was going on in the corner of the room where the instrument stood. Had he been at liberty to give the conversation his attention, he would have gathered that the speaker at the Valley Fields end was getting some disturbing news over the wire. A dark flush had come into Keggs's face, and the hand that held the receiver was shaking.

Presently Lord Uffenham, wearying of the canary – and no wonder, for it definitely lacked sustained dramatic interest –

went back to the goldfish. And he was just thinking how extra-ordinarily like one of them was to that aunt of his in Shropshire at whose house his old guv'nor had once made him go and stay, when he was jerked from his meditations by a sharp exclamation, and turned, mystified. It seemed almost inconceivable that one of Augustus Keggs's poise and dignity should have used violent language, but that was what it had sounded like.

'What did yer say?' he asked, blinking.

'I said damn and blast his eyes, m'lord,' replied Keggs respectfully.

'Eh? Who?'

'Mr Bunyan, m'lord.'

'Oh, that feller? What's he been doing?'

Keggs struggled with his emotion for a space. Then he regained self-control. A butler, toughened by years of listening to employers telling the same funny story night after night at the dinner-table, learns to master his feelings.

'It has come as a complete surprise to me, m'lord, but it appears that Mr Bunyan was engaged to be married to my niece Emma.' Here his feelings momentarily got the better of him again, and he added the words: 'Curse him! One of those secret betrothals, m'lord. Her mother learned of it only this morning.'

Lord Uffenham was mystified. He could detect nothing in the news that might have been expected to cause so pronounced a spiritual upheaval in this uncle. Most uncles, it seemed to him, knowing that Roscoe Bunyan had a matter of twenty million dollars in the old sock, would have wished that they had half his complaint.

'Engaged to yer niece, is he? Well, sooner her than me, but I should have said it was a dashed good match for the girl.

Piefaced though he is, he's well fixed. Surely you know that the feller has more money than you can shake a stick at?'

'Certainly, m'lord. Mr Bunyan must be among our wealthiest bachelors.'

'Then why are yer standing there blinding and stiffing about it?' asked Lord Uffenham, completely at a loss.

Once again the intensity of his emotions was almost too much for Augustus Keggs. It was impossible for a man of his build to sway like a daffodil in a March wind, but he unquestionably swayed to a certain extent. There was a dangerous light in his gooseberry eyes, and when he spoke it was with a guttural intonation rather like that of the bulldog George when he got a bone stuck in his throat.

'My niece Emma has just been in telephonic communication with her mother, m'lord, to inform her that Mr Bunyan has broken the engagement.'

Lord Uffenham saw all. He could understand now why this old employee of his was seething like a newly opened bottle of ginger-pop. In the other's place he, too, would have seethed. His quick sympathies were aroused.

'The dirty dog. Let yer niece Emma down, has he? Gave your niece Emma the push, did he? Odd thing is, I didn't know yer *had* a niece Emma.'

'I fancy that if I ever mentioned her to your lordship, it would have been by her *nom de tayarter*. She acts under the name of Elaine Dawn.'

'Oh, I see. On the stage, is she?'

'Precisely, m'lord, and weighing the pros and cons, she came to the conclusion that as Emma Billson she would be handicapped in her career. Something more euphonious seemed indicated.'

'Yerss, possibly she was right. Though there was Lottie Collins.'

'Yes, m'lord.'

'And Florrie Forde – and Daisy Wood. Simple enough names, those.'

'Very true, m'lord, but the ladies you mention were singers on the music halls. Emma's art is of a more serious nature. She is in what theatrical journals term the legit. When Mr Bunyan made her acquaintance, she was playing a small role in a translation from the Russian.'

'Oh, my God! An aunt of mine once made me take her to one of those. Lot of gosh-awful bounders standing around saying how sad it all was and wondering if Ivan was going to hang himself in the barn. Don't tell me that Roscoe Bunyan, a free agent, goes to see plays translated from the Russian.'

'No, m'lord. He did not witness Emma's performance. They met at a party.'

'Ah, now your story becomes more plausible. I know what happens at parties. He asked her to marry him?'

'Yes, m'lord.'

'Did he write her any letters to that effect?'

'Several, m'lord.'

'Then what's she worrying about? Lord love a duck, my dear feller, she's on velvet. She can sue him for breach of promise and skin him for millions.'

'No, m'lord.' A brief spasm shook Keggs. Of all sad words of tongue or pen, he seemed to be saying to himself, the saddest are these – It might have been. 'On going this morning to the drawer where she kept Mr Bunyan's letters, she found they had disappeared.'

'Weren't there, yer mean?'

'Precisely, m'lord. Obviously an emissary of Mr Bunyan had obtained clandestine access to her apartment in her absence and purloined the communications in question.'

It took Lord Uffenham some moments to work this out, but eventually he unravelled it and was able to translate it from the butlerese. What the man was trying to say was that some low blister, bought with Bunyan's gold, had sneaked into the girl's flat and pinched the bally things. His whole chivalrous nature was stirred to its depth by the outrage.

'The louse!'

'Yes, m'lord.'

'The ruddy Tishbite!'

'Yes, m'lord.'

'She mustn't take this lying down.'

'It is difficult to see what redress the unhappy girl can have.'

'She could dot him in the eye.'

'It would be but a poor palliative for her distress of mind.'

'Well, *someone* ought to dot him in the eye. Wait!' said Lord Uffenham, holding up a hamlike hand. 'An idea's coming. Let me think.' He paced the room for awhile. It was plain that that great brain was working. 'Hey!' he said, halting in mid-stride.

'M'lord?'

'Didn't yer tell me once that that brother-in-law of yours used to be a professional scrapper?'

'Yes, m'lord. He fought under the sobriquet of Battling Billson.'

'Good, was he? Tough sort of bloke?'

'Very, m'lord. I have a photograph of him, if your lordship would care to glance at it.'

He went to a cupboard under the window and returned with a large album. Turning pages adorned with photographs – here an impressionistic study of himself as a callow young footman, there a snapshot of a stout lady heavily swathed in the bathing costume of the eighteen-nineties, labelled 'Cousin Amy at Llandudno' – he came at last to the one he sought.

It was plainly a wedding group. Beside a chair, dressed in billowy white, stood a buxom girl with hair like a bird's nest and 'barmaid' written all over her. In her left hand she held a bouquet of liles of the valley, her right she rested lovingly on the shoulder of the man who was sitting in the chair.

The first thing the beholder noticed about this man was his size. Lord Uffenham was no pigmy, but beside the bridegroom in this photograph he would have seemed one. The fellow bestrode the narrow chair like a colossus. Impressed by his bulk and turning to a closer scrutiny, the eye was then arrested by his face, which was even more formidable. He had a broken nose, his jaw was the jaw of the star of a Western B-picture registering Determination, and beneath that wedding frock coat one could discern the rippling muscles. He was sitting with a clenched fist on each thigh, bending forward slightly as if to get a better view of an opponent across the ring. The whole effect was that of a boxer waiting for the opening bell, with his manager – female in this case – giving him a last pep talk before he came out fighting. It impressed Lord Uffenham profoundly.

'That's him, is it? The wench's father?'

'Yes, m'lord.'

'Then I see daylight,' said Lord Uffenham. 'I see where we go from here.'

The morning following Pilbeam's visit to Castlewood found Roscoe Bunyan in radiant spirits. A telephone call from the private investigator as he breakfasted had informed him that the latter's mission had been carried out according to plan and it was with a light heart that he stepped on the accelerator of his Jaguar and started off for London.

Giving his name to the gentlemanly office boy in the outer room, he was ushered without delay into the Pilbeam sanctum, and found the proprietor of the Argus Inquiry Agency seated at his desk, busy with papers of private eyeful interest. He looked up as his visitor entered, but there was no reflection in his aspect of the sunniness which was filling Roscoe. He was austere and cold.

'Oh, it's you?' he said distantly.

'Yes, here I am,' said Roscoe, marvelling not a little that on this morning of mornings the pimpled bloodhound should not have got more of the holiday spirit.

'A nice thing you let me in for yesterday,' said Pilbeam, shivering for a moment, as memory did its work. 'You told me that house would be empty.'

'Wasn't it?'

'No, it was *not*. Let me tell you what happened.'

The ability to tell a good story well is not given to all, but it was one which his fairy godmothers had bestowed on Percy Pilbeam in full measure. Nothing could have been clearer or more dramatic than his *résumé* of the Saturday afternoon's doings in that house of terror, Castlewood, Mulberry Grove, Valley Fields. It was like something particularly vivid from the pages of Edgar Allan Poe. And though both Lord Uffenham and Mortimer Bayliss might have taken exception to his description of their physical peculiarities and their behaviour, even they would have had to admit that the picture he drew was an impressive one.

When he had finished, Roscoe agreed that all that could not have been at all pleasant, and Pilbeam said no, it had not been. Thrice in the night, he said, he had woken up shaking like a jelly, having dreamed that the ordeal was still in progress.

'Still,' said Roscoe, indicating the bright side, 'you got the paper.'

'I did,' said Pilbeam. *'And* read it.'

Roscoe started violently.

'You mean you opened the envelope?'

'That's what I mean.'

'Well, you had no right to.'

Percy Pilbeam lowered the pen with which he had been combing the eastern end of his moustache.

'Sue me,' he said briefly.

There was a rather tense silence for a moment. But Roscoe was feeling too uplifted to brood for long on this lapse from professional etiquette.

'Oh, well, I don't suppose it matters,' he said, remembering that the bill had already been paid. 'Where is it?'

'In the safe.'

'Gimme.'

'Certainly,' said Pilbeam, 'as soon as you have given me your cheque for two thousand pounds.'

Roscoe reeled.

'What!'

'You should buy one of these hearing aids. Two thousand pounds, I said.'

'But I paid you.'

'And now you're going to pay me again.'

'But you promised me you would do the job for a thousand.'

'And you promised me,' said Pilbeam coldly, 'that there would be nobody in that house but Keggs and a sick bulldog. Sick bulldog, my left foot. The place was congested with hulking human hippopotami and men with spades, and they wanted to take my clothes off and paint me black. Naturally, our original agreement, made under the supposition that I would have a clear field, is null and void. The extra two thousand is for moral and intellectual damage, and I'm going to have it.'

'That's what you think.'

'That's what I know.'

'You do, do you?'

'Yes, I do.'

'I won't give you a cent,' said Roscoe.

Pilbeam, who during these exchanges had suspended the curling of his moustache, took up the pen again and ran it meditatively through the undergrowth, attending this time to the moustache's western aspect. He looked at Roscoe reproachfully, and one could see that his trust in the fundamental goodness of human nature had been shaken.

'So after all I went through to save you from having to give Keggs a hundred thousand dollars,' he said, 'you refuse to pay me a measly two thousand pounds?'

'That's right,' said Roscoe.

Pilbeam sighed, a disillusioned man.

'Well, suit yourself,' he said resignedly. 'I've no doubt Keggs will think the paper worth that to him.'

The room swam before Roscoe's eyes. He seemed to be seeing the other through a flickering mist which obscured his outlines and made him almost invisible. But, though anyone would have told him that that was much the pleasantest way of seeing Percy Pilbeam, he drew no comfort from this.

'You wouldn't do that?'

'Who says so?'

'You'd give it to Keggs?'

'*Sell* it to Keggs,' corrected Pilbeam. 'I'm sure I should find him a good customer. A level-headed sort of man he seemed to me.'

'This is blackmail!'

'I know. Criminal offence. There's the 'phone, if you want to call the police.'

'Keggs'll do that. He'll have you arrested.'

'And lose a hundred thousand dollars? He won't have me arrested. He'll lay down the red carpet for me.'

Roscoe had shot his bolt. He had gone out of his class, he realized, and had come up against an intelligence so superior that he was as a child in its presence. There seemed to him nothing to do but to accept defeat as gracefully as possible.

Then there flashed into his mind a healing thought. Cheques could be stopped.

'All right,' he said, 'you win.' He drew out the cheque-book which was his constant companion. 'May I borrow your pen?'

Pilbeam removed the pen from the hair on top of his head, to which some minutes ago he had transferred it.

'Here you are. And now,' he said, taking the cheque, 'I'll just ask you to come with me to the bank while I cash this. They won't pay a large sum like two thousand pounds across the counter without your okay. And then we'll come back and I'll give you that paper and we'll all be happy.'

It would be an overstatement to say that Roscoe, as he drove back to Shipley Hall half an hour later, was happy, but by the time he turned in at the Hall's gates the bitter cup, to which his lips were becoming so accustomed these days, had begun to taste a little better. Nothing, of course, could make the expenditure of two thousand pounds actually enjoyable, but by concentrating his mind on the fact that the Keggs-Bunyan contract was now a little pile of ashes in Percy Pilbeam's waste-paper basket he was able to bear up. If all was not for the best in this best of all possible worlds, it was at any rate considerably better than it might have been. A glance at the score sheet showed him that he was well ahead of the game. He would have preferred not to have been compelled to go in quite so largely for sprats, but the salient point that emerged was that he had caught the whale.

He braked the Jaguar at the front door, and went into the house. Skidmore was in the hall.

'A Mr and Mrs Billson have called, sir,' said Skidmore.

CHAPTER 25

Ever since rising from his bed that morning, Mortimer Bayliss had been feeling depressed and irritable. Most unwisely, when replacing the spade in the flower bed, he had dug a few tentative digs with it, and this had brought on an attack of lumbago, causing him to look on life with a jaundiced eye. It was one of those reminders, which came so frequently nowadays, that he was not as young as he had been, and he resented anything that interfered with his mental picture of himself as a sprightly juvenile. As he stood in the gallery at Shipley Hall, staring moodily at one of the works of Sidney Biffen's middle period, there floated into his mind the sombre words of Walter Savage Landor:

> I warmed both hands before the fire of life.
> It sinks, and I am ready to depart

and suddenly there came upon him the realization that he could not endure another day of Roscoe Bunyan's society.

Business connected with the Bunyan Collection had brought him to Shipley, but that business being now concluded there was no reason why he should continue to be cooped up with one whom he had disliked as a boy and disliked even more heartily now that a too tolerant world had permitted him to survive to

the age of thirty-one. Everything about Roscoe offended him –
his face, his double chin, his conversation and his habit of
employing private investigators to the undoing of fiancées and
ex-butlers.

For it was clear to him, now that he had had time to think
it over, that the hand of Roscoe had been behind yesterday's
incursion into Castlewood of that striped-suited marauder with
the moustache. It had puzzled him at the time why any burglar,
unless fond of goldfish and aspidistras, should have thought
it worth his while to burgle Keggs's living-room, but if one
assumed him to have been a minion of Roscoe's, hired by
Roscoe to make away with that contract, his actions became
intelligible.

Roscoe, he felt, was a man in whose presence it was impossible
for a self-respecting art expert to go on breathing, and he was
hobbling to the bell to ring it, with a view to starting his preparations for leaving, when Skidmore appeared.

'Excuse me, sir,' said Skidmore. 'Could you see Mr Keggs?'

A flicker of interest lightened the gloom of Mortimer Bayliss's
gnarled face. Augustus Keggs was the one person whose society
at the moment he felt equal to tolerating. They had much to talk
about together.

'Is he here?'

'He arrived some little while ago in his car, sir, with a lady and
gentleman.'

'Then send him up. And pack.'

'Sir?'

'My belongings, oaf.'

'You are leaving Shipley Hall, sir?'

'I am. It stinks, and I am ready to depart.'

When Keggs entered, nursing his bowler hat, his aspect smote

Mortimer Bayliss like a blow. Misery loves company, and he had been looking forward to getting together with a fellow-invalid with whom he could swap symptoms. To see the man in glowing health – positively rosy, in fact – was a sad disappointment.

'You seem to have recovered,' he said sourly. 'I should have thought you would have had a headache this morning.'

'Oh, no, sir.'

'No, headache?'

'No, sir, thank you. I am in excellent fettle.'

'Too bad. Ouch!'

'You are feeling unwell, sir?'

'Crick in the back. Lumbago.'

'A painful ailment.'

'Most. But never mind about me. Nobody ever does. I have yet to meet the man who gives a damn what happens to poor old Bayliss. If I were being torn limb from limb by a homicidal gorilla and a couple of fellows who knew me came along, one of them would say "Don't look now, but Mortimer Bayliss is over there being torn limb from limb by a gorilla", and the other would reply "You're absolutely right. So he is", and they would go off to lunch. Well, what brings you here, Keggs? Yesterday's excitement in the home?'

'My visit is connected with that, yes, sir.'

'I suppose when you came out of your swoon, you found the contract gone and realized that the boy friend had swiped it on behalf of Roscoe?'

'Immediately, sir.'

'And now you have come to plead with him to do the square thing and give you at least a little something of his plenty? Not a hope, my good Keggs, not a hope. Conscience will never make Roscoe part with a nickel.'

'So I had anticipated, sir. It was not with any intention of appealing to Mr Bunyan's better feelings that I made the journey here. I came to escort my sister and her husband, who are now closeted with Mr Bunyan in the smoking-room. It was Lord Uffenham's suggestion that I should bring them here for a conference. They are the parents of the young woman to whom Mr Bunyan was until recently betrothed. My niece Emma.'

'What on earth do you suppose they can do?'

'His lordship was sanguine that a visit from them would accomplish something in the nature of a desirable settlement.'

A kindly, almost tender look came into the eye behind Mortimer Bayliss's black-rimmed monocle. He was feeling a gentle pity for this man who seemed so completely out of touch with the facts of life.

'But, Keggs,' he said, and there was a pleading note in his voice, the sort of note that creeps into a man's voice when he is trying to reason with the half-witted, 'the minion who stole that contract of yours also stole the letters Roscoe wrote to the girl, promising marriage. She's as helpless as you are.'

Keggs shook his head, a thing which before visiting the wizard of Rosendale Road he could not have done without causing it to split into two equal halves and shoot up to the ceiling.

'His lordship was inclined to think not. He took the view that Wilberforce—'

'Eh?'

'My brother-in-law, sir. His lordship took the view that Wilberforce might conceivably persuade Mr Bunyan to change his mind and do the right thing by our Emma. And he was not astray in his judgment. When I left them a moment ago, Mr Bunyan had quite come round to the idea of an immediate wedding.'

It took a good deal, as has been shown, to dislodge the monocle from Mortimer Bayliss's eye, but at these words it shot from its base and leaped at the end of its string like a lamb gambolling in Springtime.

'He had . . . *what*?'

'Sir?'

'Come round to the idea of an immediate wedding, did you say? He's going to marry the girl?'

'By special licence.'

'In spite of having got back the letters?'

'Precisely, sir.'

Mortimer Bayliss hauled in the slack and replaced the monocle in his eye. It was almost an unconscious reflex action, for he was feeling dazed.

'Your brother-in-law must be very eloquent,' he said.

Keggs smiled a gentle smile.

'I would not call him that, sir. He seldom speaks. My sister Flossie does all the talking for the family. But Wilberforce was at one time a professional boxer, operating in the heavyweight division.'

A gleam of light penetrated Mortimer Bayliss's darkness. Dimly he began to see.

'Battling Billson was the name under which he appeared in the roped arena. He is a little elderly now, of course, but still vigorous. At his public house in Shoreditch the clientele, as is so often the way with the proletariat in the East End of London, is inclined to become obstreperous towards closing time, and my sister tells me that Wilberforce thinks nothing of engaging in combat half a dozen or more costermongers or representatives of the Merchant Marine simultaneously, always with complete success. His left hook, I understand, still functions as effectively as in his prime. And no doubt his mere appearance carried weight with Mr Bunyan.'

'Formidable, is it?'

'Extremely, sir. If one may employ the vernacular, he looks a killer.'

A feeling of quiet happiness was stealing over Mortimer Bayliss. For years, he was telling himself, Roscoe Bunyan had been asking for something along these lines, and now he had got it.

'So those wedding bells will ring out?'

'Yes, sir.'

'When?'

'Immediately, sir.'

'Well, that's fine. I congratulate you.'

'Thank you, sir. I have never been fond of Mr Roscoe myself, but it is pleasant to think that my niece's future is provided for.'

'How much would you say Roscoe has? Twenty million dollars?'

'About that, I should imagine, sir.'

'Nice money.'

'Extremely nice, sir. Emma will like having it at her disposal. And there was one other thing.'

'What's that?'

'I have drawn up a fresh contract to take the place of the one purloined from my apartment. Flossie, when I left the smoking-room, was just going into the matter with Mr Bunyan and by this time I have no doubt will have overcome any reluctance on his part to sign such a document. If you would be kind enough to come to the smoking-room and witness it, as before, I should be greatly obliged. It is possible,' said Keggs, forestalling an anticipated objection, 'that you may be thinking that, with Mr Roscoe planning to enter upon matrimony at so early a date, the contract will be valueless, marriage automatically ruling him out of the tontine. But I have a suggestion which I fancy would make things satisfactory for all parties concerned.'

'You have?'

'Yes, sir. Why should not Mr Bunyan and Mr Hollister agree to divide the proceeds of the tontine equally, irrespective of which is the first to marry?'

There was something in Mortimer Bayliss's aspect of the watcher of the skies when a new planet swims into his ken. He started, and for a moment sat in silence, as if savouring the suggestion.

'That never occurred to me,' he said.

'Mr Bunyan, as I see it, would have no option but to agree. No doubt Mr Hollister is anxious to embark on matrimony at as early a date as possible, but he would scarcely be unwilling to postpone the ceremony for the few days which will elapse before Mr Roscoe's wedding takes place. This could be pointed out to Mr Roscoe.'

'I'll point it out to him myself.'

'It would be a simple matter to draw up a contract binding on both gentlemen.'

'Perfectly simple.'

'And each would find it equally advantageous. Really, sir, I can see no flaw. It seems to solve everything.'

'It does. In the smoking-room, did you say your loved ones were?'

'Yes, sir.'

'Then let's join them. I am particularly anxious to see this brother-in-law of yours, whose mere aspect has had so hypnotic an effect on our Mr Bunyan. I can hardly wait. Good Lord!'

'Sir?'

'I was only thinking that if this girl he's marrying is your niece, Roscoe will have to go through life calling you Uncle Joe or whatever it is.'

'Uncle Gussie, sir.'

Mortimer Bayliss flung his arms up in a gesture of ecstasy. The sudden movement gave him a nasty twinge in the small of the back, but he ignored it.

'This,' he said, 'is the maddest, merriest day of all the glad new year. I do believe in fairies! I do!'

There are clubs in London where talk is as the crackling of thorns under a pot and it is *de rigueur* to throw lumps of sugar across the room at personal friends, and other, more sedate clubs where silence reigns and the inmates curl up in armchairs, close their eyes and leave the rest to Nature. Lord Uffenham's was one of the latter. In its smoking-room this afternoon there were present, besides his lordship and Mortimer Bayliss, some dozen living corpses, all breathing gently with their eyes closed and letting the world go by. A travelled observer, entering, would have been forcibly reminded of seals basking on rocks or alligators taking it easy in some tropical swamp.

The eyes of Lord Uffenham and his guest were at the moment open, but the eyelids were a little weary and both were feeling in need of rest and repose. It taxes the energies of elderly gentlemen to attend a wedding, kiss the bride, and stand waving as the receding car takes the young couple off on their honeymoon. Like the gardenias in their buttonholes, these two were more than a trifle wilted.

Lord Uffenham, moreover, in addition to being physically fatigued, was mentally in a state of turmoil. Recent happenings had left him dazed and bewildered. He was able vaguely to gather that young Fred Holloway, who had hitched up with his niece Jane, had become possessed of approximately half a million dollars, and that of course was all to the good, for he had been assured by Jane that he, Lord Uffenham, was to have his share of these pennies from heaven, but how this very agreeable state of affairs had come about he did not begin to understand. All day he had been bending his brain to the problem and trying to make sense of the explanations which had been given him by Jane, by Bill, by Keggs and by Mortimer Bayliss, and this had made him feel drowsy.

It was consequently only a fleeting attention that he was able to accord to the observations of his companion, who, though also conscious of a certain exhaustion, was talking as fluently as usual.

'Weddings,' said Mortimer Bayliss, drawing thoughtfully at his cigar, 'always cheer me up. Why is that, Bayliss? I'll tell you. They give me that feeling of quiet satisfaction which comes to an explorer in the jungle who sees the boa-constrictor swallow the other fellow, and not him. I look at the bridegroom and I say to myself "Well, they've got that poor mutt, Mortimer, but they haven't got you, Mort, old sport", and my heart leaps up as if I had beheld a rainbow in the sky. Are you awake?'

'M-m-m-m-m,' said Lord Uffenham.

'Mind you, I am quite aware, of course, that there are eccentrics who enjoy getting married. The recent Hollister, for instance, was obviously feeling no qualms as they sprang the trap on him. He gloried in his predicament. But, as I was telling you the other day, I have always regarded the holy state with the gravest concern. As a young man, I would sometimes dream that I was being married, and would wake sweating. But each year that passes lessens the peril, and my mind is now tolerably easy. I look at myself in the mirror and I say "Courage! With a face like that you are surely safe, Mortimer." It is a most consoling thought. Are you still awake?'

Lord Uffenham did not reply. He was breathing gently.

'Because, if so, I would like your ruling on a point which has been exercising my mind not a little. Bill Hollister. Would you say that he was one of those honourable young men with rigid ethical standards, not – in short – the sort of young man to stick to money to which he was not entitled, as would be the case with so many of us, like a mustard plaster?'

Lord Uffenham breathed gently.

'That is the impression he has always given me, and I cannot, therefore, but feel that it would be injudicious to let him know the true facts about that matrimonial tontine of mine – to wit, that his father was never in it. You amaze me, Bayliss, tell me more. Certainly. I was just going to. As I told Roscoe when the whole thing started, one of those dining at J. J. Bunyan's table on that September night in the year 1929 changed his mind next morning and decided to include himself out. That one was Bill's late father. He said he thought the whole idea damned silly and nobody was going to get fifty thousand dollars of his money for nonsense of that sort. In other words, to make it clear to the meanest intelligence – I allude to yours, my dear Uffenham – Roscoe has paid out half a million dollars he didn't have to, in addition to a hundred thousand to Keggs, twenty thousand pounds to Stanhope Twine, and I imagine, a princely sum to that minion with the pimples. A consummation devoutly to be wished, of course, for, as I have sometimes pointed out, it will make him more spiritual, and he is a man who needs all the spirituality he can get, but a state of affairs at which Bill Hollister, if I read him aright, would look askance. I consider it a certainty that the young sap, if apprised, will insist on handing the stuff back, so the view I take is that he must not be apprised. As the phrase is, he must never know. Sealed lips. I say. What do you say?'

Lord Uffenham did not say anything. He had begun to snore softly, and it became plain to Mortimer Bayliss that of all this nicely reasoned speech he had heard not a single word.

And better so, felt Mortimer Bayliss, far better so. This top secret was one to be locked, if possible, in a single bosom. Viscounts sometimes babble. When in their cups, for instance. He did not know if Lord Uffenham was ever in his cups, but it was quite possible that he might some day chance to get into them and with an unloosened tongue speak the injudicious word.

Sealed lips, thought Mortimer Bayliss, sealed lips. You can't beat sealed lips.

He laid down his cigar. He leaned back in his chair. His eyes closed. And presently his gentle breathing blended with Lord Uffenham's gentle breathing and the gentle breathing of all the other basking alligators in the Mausoleum Club's smoking-room.

He slept, the good man taking his rest after a busy day.

TITLES IN THE COLLECTOR'S WODEHOUSE

This edition of P. G. Wodehouse has been prepared from the first British printing of each title.

The Collector's Wodehouse is printed on acid-free paper and set in Caslon, a typeface designed and engraved by William Caslon of William Caslon & Son, Letter-Founders in London around 1740.